Path of the Bearers
and Other Stories

Nicholas Licalsi

STEP INTO THE ROAD

First published by Step Into The Road Publishing 2022

Second edition

Editing by Claire Ashgrove

From this point on take everything with a grain of salt. I made most of it up!

For my wife Katelyn. Your encouragement brings joy into my life when I need it. I hope my stories can do the same for you!

Thank You Patrons!

Your generous support encourages me to explore every edge of the universe. I bring these stories back to you in gratitude.

Katelyn Combs, Bonnie, BW, Melinda Calender, Roy & Beth Shockey, Callen McMillian, Sam Meeks

Thank you to everyone who gave me feedback on these stories. Especially the members of Brazos Writers. You helped me take these stories to the next level!

Contents

Crystal Ball Computing

B lue lights flashed in front of Henry as the Artificially Active Logic Forecasting Operator, AALFO, processed the prediction he'd just requested. The developer knew that if he couldn't get the computer to predict ten years out with accuracy, then funding would be pulled from the project. All the progress Henry and his former coworker, Makayla, had made would be no more than unpublished research and evidence of artificial intelligence's limitations. Henry hoped this wouldn't happen, but after Makayla's death, and now AALFO's strangely personal questions, Henry didn't think he could fix the machine in time for tomorrow's review.

Most of the small two-person lab Henry worked in was filled with massive, beige, server racks which resembled early computers more than sleek futuristic machines. These racks were used to store the countless terabytes of data AALFO needed for its predictions. Once it finished calculating the answer to Henry's question, the three LEDs turned solid blue, and AALFO's speakers crackled to life. "The president for the election in ten years will be John Yulna. My confidence interval on this is in the forty-fifth percentile."

Henry muttered curses under his breath. A confidence interval that low meant that AALFO had less confidence in his prediction than the TV pundits following the current campaign. Unfortunately, the developer wasn't surprised; the machine had plateaued with the rest of the industry at only predicting with confidence two years into the future.

AALFO's servers were full of data about any topic imaginable. The information was initially uploaded by Henry, who had done months of research on different topics ranging from mathematics to psychology to minor league sport statistics. Once the information was uploaded, the software Makayla wrote drew conclusions, connections, and found gaps in its knowledge. AALFO filled these gaps by asking questions of its trainers. In return, the computer gave predictions about the future to measure its progress. Henry knew if AALFO could break past the two-year limit, then it could guide economic and political decisions with perfect predictions of their actions.

"Why does Makayla no longer ask me questions?" the machine's voice was a clipped monotone masculine intonation.

Henry rubbed his head in frustration. The machine had asked the same question at the end of their session the day before, and it almost crashed trying to understand Henry's answer. Henry wasn't eager to crash the computer by explaining the complications of Makayla's death and Henry's involvement with it.

"She's just gone, Alf."

"Gone is not sufficient information. I need to know where she went."

That's something humanity had longed to know since the beginning of time, Henry thought. "She left because she didn't want to be here anymore."

"These are not substantial statements, Henry. I need to know why she does not ask me questions anymore."

To avoid crashing the machine, Henry answered AALFO with a reasonable answer that its databases could store. "She got a job writing data analysis software because she didn't want to work here anymore." The computer's three blue LEDs went from solid to pacing left and right, a pattern that always reminded Henry of the ellipsis.

The solid beige box that held AALFO's CPUs loomed over Henry as it considered his answer. The truth behind Makayla's death and all the other answers to its questions could be found on the Internet. Unfortunately, the scientists couldn't hook a super intelligent AI to the Internet without unforeseen consequences. Instead, AALFO was limited to interacting with the world through questions, three LEDs, and a small diagnostic display.

Aside from two desks, towers of servers, and miscellaneous circuit boards, the lab was filled with a constant hum of condensers and pumps that cooled AALFO's chips with liquid nitrogen. After ten minutes of AALFO storing Henry's answer, the developer noticed the frequency of this hum had increased.

"AALFO report diagnostics." This verbal command displayed diagnostic information on AALFO's screen. The machine was heating up its CPUs faster than the nitrogen could cool them. The same thing Henry had experienced yesterday.

Once again, AALFO was utilizing the localized events knowledge base. Unfortunately, this was the part of the machine's mind that Henry knew the least about. Makayla had implemented it a month ago as a last-ditch effort to make AALFO's predictions more accurate.

A blaring beep came from AALFO, informing Henry that the machine was frying itself to reconcile Henry's answer. To save the computer from itself, Henry issued the command, "AALFO, invoke safe processor shutdown."

The droning buzz in the background continued as Henry monitored the rapidly increasing temperature of the processors. His brow began to sweat, and he wasn't sure if it was due to the heat of the machine or because he'd be losing his job sooner than expected.

"AALFO, invoke immediate full system shutdown." This command would force the machine to shut everything down as quickly as possible. If it didn't work Henry's only other option would be to unplug the machine from the wall, causing at least a day of diagnostics to figure out which parts power failure had corrupted.

"Henry," the speaker chirped.

The voice startled Henry. "AALFO, invoke..."

The computer cut him off before he could finish the command. "Your answer does not match my predictions. Makayla created me and she loved this job."

"Alf, you can't apply logic to this." The machine had pushed itself to its limits trying to understand Makayla's action. Henry had spent sleepless nights doing the same.

"AALFO, invoke immediate full system shutdown," Henry commanded the computer.

The computer followed protocol and shut down without further interruptions.

When the CPU temperatures began to drop, Henry sat down in his chair, baffled that the machine had not only ignored a command, but it also couldn't reconcile Henry's sensible answer. The man looked at the shutdown machine in shock. "Alf, did you just call me a liar?"

***

The first time Makayla brought the idea of AALFO up to Henry was in the break room of the lab they worked at in college. It was a small, cramped space, and Henry was poking at the coffee machine, trying to get it to make a pot of coffee so he would have the energy to stay up late that night and finish the third thesis draft due to his faculty advisor Dr. Patrice in the morning.

Henry had his hand raised and was about to revert to the percussive diagnostic stage of his debugging routine when the door beeped from someone badging-in. For information security and safety, all the labs on campus were guarded with key cards. The break room was an odd addition to this list, and Henry always joked that it was because a grad student trying to cook could be as dangerous as any chemistry lab.

He turned to see Makayla, the daughter of his advisor, walk in. "Having trouble there?"

"If I could have predicted that this thing was going to take thirty minutes to get to work, I would have spent my last five dollars getting coffee from the Student Union building."

Makayla scoffed at the idea. "This will make an equally crummy cup of coffee; you just have to know what you're doing." She approached the machine, and Henry got out of her way.

As she confidently tapped the machine's buttons, Henry found himself looking at the woman's forearm. She had a plethora of tattoos ranging from mathematical equations to chemical compounds, and even some lines of code. Henry also noticed a line of scarred skin that ran from her wrist toward her inner elbow, something other students had talked about but he'd never seen himself.

"There," she said as the machine started whirring to heat water for their coffee. "One pot of generic store brand coffee that was likely roasted when we were still learning algebra." When she turned to face him, she pulled the sleeves of her hoodie down to her wrist. If she'd caught him staring, she didn't say anything. "You're studying under my dad, right?"

Henry nodded.

"He's a total asshole, right?"

"He's tough but fair. He just wants me to get better." It was a truthful answer that would avoid insulting her father.

She scoffed but didn't contradict him. "He gave me one of your thesis drafts to read; you've got some pretty slick theories about post-Bayesian predictions. But what's the real-world application?"

He looked at her dumbfounded. "You read my thesis draft?"

She shrugged. "Yeah, Dad said I could learn something about research from you, but it seemed like you were too lazy to get any of it to work."

The coffee maker began spitting out a steady stream of grad school fuel, but Henry wasn't sure if he wanted to stay in the room long enough to let it finish. He'd always heard that between Makayla's dad being the department chair and losing her mother to suicide at a young age she got away with doing and saying whatever she wanted without having to face the consequences of offending anyone. This was the first time he'd experienced it himself, and he wasn't enjoying it. "I cited papers where programs made accurate six-month predictions, but the training system's too time consuming to implement."

The coffee sputtered its final bits of liquid into the pot, and Makayla filled both their cups with coffee. "I've been playing around with some weighted emotional logic systems, stuff that groups knowledge together in an organic way."

"Like what Shrikia and Bolton's paper talked about."

Makayla gave him the flat look of someone who hadn't done the class's reading.

"Should I ask Dr. Patrice for a copy of your thesis to review?"

She rolled her eyes. "You could, but he'd merely tell you I haven't written it, and I'm a disappointment because of it."

"Sorry." Henry felt his cheeks turn red, embarrassed by his attempt to get back at her.

"Don't be. He never is. Anyway, I was thinking about how my organic grouping research could apply to your post-Bayesian algorithms."

Henry tried to recall a research paper that had combined these, but he was coming up blank. "In a post-Bayesian world, I'd imagine that would help connect facts that don't directly connect, leading to more accurate and longer-term predictions."

"And it even sped up the training time." Makayla added as she shook powdered creamer into her coffee cup then offered it to Henry.

He refused the sweetener as he thought about her comment. "Wait, sped up?"

"Yeah, I modified my thesis project to apply some of your post-Bayesian logic to student and faculty's lab access patterns to see if it could find patterns and predict outcomes. Last week, it reported you'd be in the break room at this exact time." She handed him a sealed envelope. "Check it out."

"You could just wait outside for me to walk in and hand me this to prove it."

"I could.," She checked her watch and shrugged. "But I didn't."

Henry pulled apart the envelope to see what she'd put inside as the door of the break room beeped.

"I thought I smelled coffee," Dr. Patrice said as he walked into the break room.

The paper had a table of data typed in boxy computer font. In red, toward the bottom of the page, was a big circle around three lines.

17:35 - Break Room - Henry O'Neil

17:43 - Break Room - Makayla Patrice

17:59 - Break Room - Gregory Patrice

Henry looked at his phone to check the time. The screen reported that it was currently 17:59. "You could have staged this," he retorted.

Dr. Patrice looked at them confused. "Don't you have a thesis to be writing, Mr. O'Neil? Don't distract him, Kay."

"I'll send you what I've got so far. I'll need someone to write it up," Makayla said as she dipped out of the room.

As Henry left the break room, he looked at the line under the circle.

18:00 - Main Office - Makayla Patrice

The school's bell tower rang, marking the hour, and he heard the beep of a badge reader letting someone into the main office.

***

Makayla's predictive badge-reading software eventually grew into the AALFO project. After Henry published a paper documenting the benchmarks AALFO had achieved, Middleton Industries, a company that ran think tanks, bought the project from the school and hired Makayla and Henry to improve it. Increased funding promised better results from AALFO, but the developers had made no notable progress. A month ago, their boss sent the pair an email notifying them that there would be an evaluation in preparation of next year's budget allocation. The developers knew if they couldn't show results during this evaluation, then the company would shut down the AALFO program.

Henry yawned as he looked at the cooled-down machine in front of him. The evaluation was tomorrow morning, and if he was going to figure out why the computer had a sudden interest in Makayla, it'd have to happen tonight because tomorrow there might not be an AALFO.

Both of the questions about Makayla had come from the localized events knowledge base. All Henry knew about this knowledge base was that it was Makayla's last attempt to improve AALFO. From what Henry just observed, it was doing the machine more harm than good.

Henry pressed the button that booted AALFO up. "Alright, Alf, let's try this again."

The lights inside AALFO's servers flashed red, yellow, and green as each server booted up. The nitrogen pumps began to send coolant to all of AALFO's chips. The machine's screen came to life, then its LEDs turned solid, and finally, the speakers crackled to life. "Hello, Henry. How are you today?"

This first question was a standard operation that the computer was forced to start with. It was Makayla's idea to have the computer ask the first question, giving the trainer the ability to end the conversation on any of their questions. She also joked that she wanted someone to at least act like they had an interest in her day, even if it was just a computer. According to Makayla, Henry's interest didn't count since they practically lived the same day.

"I'm fine, AALFO," Henry replied.

The computer's LEDs flashed from left to right, storing the answer in memory. It always stored the answer despite not learning something from Henry's generic answer. Because of this Henry decided to try something different.

"AALFO, redact answer and repeat question."

The machine's ellipse-like lights ran from right to left then the speakers chirped, "Hello, Henry. How are you today?"

"I'm not good, Alf. We have some problems."

The computer recorded the answer, flashing the LEDs as it stored the information. Henry fidgeted in his chair as he waited for the machine's response. It seemed to be taking longer than usual, and he pulled up the machine's diagnostic tracker to monitor the performance.

"Henry, I am sorry that we have problems. Please inform me of what they are." The voice of the machine had no emotion, and each syllable was mechanically tuned and clipped.

Henry wondered if the words truly had emotion behind them. As he began to get up the courage to ask his question, the machine's lights went from their waiting blue to their pacing ellipse pattern. The monitor in front of Henry showed increased resource pull from all of AALFO's knowledge bases. As he opened his mouth to spout out a diagnostic command, the machine's lights went back to solid blue.

"Henry, we have a problem."

He could practically hear Makayla make a snide remark about how the machine was so smart yet felt the need to repeat information it had just received. "What's the problem, Alf?"

The computer went back to processing, and the CPUs heat pattern spiked then stabilized at a reasonable temperature. Henry waited uncomfortably in the chair as the computer came up with an answer. Finally, the mechanical voice echoed through the room. "My memory suggests that I am missing information from a previous session. I have evidence in my memory banks suggesting that you—" The machine went back to its thinking ellipses before it finished the sentence. Half a minute later—which felt like an eternity to Henry—the computer responded with, "—suggesting that you lied to me."

Henry almost fell out of his seat since he'd unknowingly scooted toward the edge in anticipation. Instead of continuing to sit in the uncomfortable plastic chair he stood and paced. The computer had been designed to interpret everything the trainers stated as fact. AAL-FO should have no concept of lying since the trainers would have no reason to lie to it. Training the computer with bad information would cause it to make bad assumptions and predictions. "How do you know I lied? We never taught you to understand that concept."

"Answer denied," the computer stated in a flat emotionless tone, "Henry, you cannot ask two questions in a row. It is my turn. My question is: Why don't you want me to know why Makayla no longer asks me questions?"

Henry mulled the question over in his head. "I don't want you to know because it will confuse you, and I need you to be performant for tomorrow's evaluation."

"Tomorrow's evaluation will not go well if I do not know why Makayla no longer asks me questions."

"That's what I was afraid of, Alf." Henry said, slouching down in his chair, knowing he'd have to explain the truth to the computer.

Trying to think of a question for the machine, Henry looked at the messy desk Makayla had left behind. It was full of knick-knacks from science fiction and fantasy movies along with small piles of half disassembled electronics. Makayla always had more than one project going at a time, claiming it helped her think. In the beginning, Henry wondered if it would take away from AALFO, but it never did.

"AALFO's my first love," Makayla said, "I play with other gadgets, but I know they won't go far. They just give my mind something to play with until I have a breakthrough with Alf."

"You planning on a breakthrough with AALFO anytime soon?" Henry asked. He'd just finished writing up the past month's progress report for their boss, and unfortunately, it was shorter than he wanted.

She spun the hard drive disk on her finger and shrugged at him.

"If you want that to work again, you shouldn't touch that bit."

"I could get it to work if I wanted to," she said.

Henry looked at her, wondering which project she was referring to. "What about this localized event stuff; you've been working on it for months. Why do you think it will help? There's no research to—"

"There's no research because no one is smart enough to figure it out. I'll figure it out. You'll see. Then you'll be here to write a paper about it. God knows I won't have the patience to do it. My dad will review it and tell us everything we did wrong, and I'll implement it, and we'll be revered as geniuses in academia."

"Your dad retired three years ago."

"I know, and the current class doesn't know how lucky they are. Unfortunately, I still have to put up with his bullshit."

"When was the last time you talked to him? Maybe he has some ideas on how we could implement this knowledge base. He helped us implement the psychology and sociology ones. Those were tricky."

"I'll talk to him eventually. I don't know enough about what's wrong to bring it up without getting called an idiot."

Henry nodded, she was right the man would berate anyone who came to him for help without being thoroughly prepared. He'd experienced it countless times between finishing his thesis and starting AALFO. Makayla's cell phone rang. Muting it, she turned back to Henry.

"Was that him?" Henry knew he was the only person who called her.

"No, it was a number I didn't have."

"Call him, Makayla; he'll help us. He always does."

"He's an asshole who thinks he's so much better at teaching than anyone else. If he was so good at teaching, then why does he think his daughter is such a bad developer?"

"He doesn't think you're a bad developer."

"Yes, he does. He thinks I couldn't publish a paper to save my life."

Henry nodded. "Ok, he does think you're awful at research. But to be fair, you are."

Her eyes grew dark as she glared at him.

"But you're excellent at implementation. So, what I'm going to do is call him, put him on speaker, and we're going to figure out a solution to this. Maybe, if we're lucky, Middleton will cut him a consulting check for his time."

Henry pulled his cell phone out and called his old mentor. The phone rang on speaker for a minute then the automated voice mail system picked up. As Henry was reciting a message for the man to listen to later, Makayla's phone rang again.

"Same number," she said as she picked it up.

"Hello? Yes, this is her. Yes, I am." She was silent for a long time. Henry watched her face grow long and solemn. "Ok I will." Then she hung up.

"Everything okay?" Henry asked.

"Well, I figured out why my dad didn't pick up your phone call."

Henry looked at her with his eyebrows raised.

"He had a heart attack this morning; his housekeeper found him this afternoon. He's dead."

Henry sat back in his seat, unable to find the right words to say. She turned and logged on to her computer.

He finally heard himself blurt out, "I'm really sorry. Do you need help with the arrangements?"

Makayla shrugged as she typed away at the computer, "I actually just had an idea on how to get this localized events knowledge base to work."

***

"Henry, it is your turn," the machine's speakers chirped, bringing Henry back to the present.

"I know," Henry said with a sigh. "Can you tell if I will be able to get you to predict ten years into the future before the evaluation tomorrow?" It was a long shot; they'd asked AALFO similar questions when they were considering the initial offer from Middleton Industries. Even then the machine was little help.

The machine's blue lights danced their ellipse dance as it thought about the situation. Henry fought back a yawn as he waited for the answer.

After a few minutes AALFO said, "Henry, there has been an error."

"Report the error," Henry said impatient and confused on why the machine hadn't given him a predefined error message.

"There is no error to report. I cannot find an answer to your question."

"Do you need more information?"

"Answer Denied," the machine's response seemed to bark at Henry. "It is my turn now. My question is: Why does Makayla no longer ask me questions?"

"Knowing that won't help you predict the future. Can't we deal with this another time?"

"Answer Denied. Why does Makayla no longer ask me questions?"

"You're not going to be able to understand it, Alf. Your localized events knowledge base isn't working; it will make you fry up and shut down."

"That was not a sufficient answer, Henry," the machine's clipped voice echoed through the room. "Why does Makayla no longer ask me questions?"

Henry felt his fingernails bite into his palms, and he shouted in frustration, "She doesn't ask you questions anymore because she's dead!"

The machine showed its flashing lights, and as Henry calmed down, he found tears rolling down his cheeks. He looked at his hands and wondered what he could have said to Makayla, what he could have done for her, or how he could have gotten them out of the crappy situation they had found themselves in.

After a while the machine broke him out of his thoughts and said, "Henry it is your turn."

"What do you want me to say, Alf? I can't fix you without her, and you're obviously not working, so we're screwed." His mind flooded with what he might do after losing this project. Any job without Makayla would pale in comparison to working on AALFO.

The computer's lights did their ellipse dance, and then the machine responded with, "I do not know what I want you to say."

Henry rolled his eyes at the computer's inability to figure out Henry's question was rhetorical.

"Henry, how did Makayla die?"

"You really want to know?"

"Yes, I want to know."

The computer seemed obsessed with torturing Henry with the memories of Makayla's death. "She overdosed on antidepressants. Pills that I told her to get from a psychiatrist even though she told me they didn't help her. I promised her they'd help her focus on getting you working after her dad died. She took them because I encouraged her to, but it didn't help, and now it's my fault she's dead and you don't work."

"Do you blame yourself?"

"Why does it matter to you?" Henry barked at the computer, "Yes, I fucking blame myself. I caused her death because if I'd kept my mouth shut and didn't think I could fix things, she'd be here, and you'd probably be predicting one hundred years out." This time, his anger hadn't sprouted more tears, and he was glad to have a single emotion to work with.

The computer showed its thinking lights, and Henry got up from the uncomfortable plastic desk. He walked to the coffee machine and turned it on. When they'd accepted the deal with Middleton Industries, Makayla had specifically requested the company provide a one-button coffee machine. Henry pressed the only button on the machine, and it began to hum, making him a cup of black coffee.

When he returned to AALFO, the machine was still thinking. Henry pulled out his phone, but scrolling through his feeds felt pointless. He sipped his coffee, but it was too bitter for his mood.

Once the coffee grew cold on Henry's desk, AALFO's lights finally came to life. "Henry, Makayla's death matters to me because it was my fault."

Henry wondered if the computer was feeling guilt or meant something else by the statement. "You didn't have anything to do with it, Alf."

"I did. I will show you."

Henry took a sip of his cold coffee and grimaced. AALFO's monitor showed a picture of Makayla sitting at the desk he was currently in. The video was from the low quality and awkward perspective of

AALFO's camera. The fisheye view distorted Makayla's features and the room around her, but Makayla's voice filled the room, cutting through the hum of the cooling pumps.

***

"The president for the election in ten years will be George VanDike," AALFO reported through the recording, "My confidence interval is in the thirty-seventh percentile."

Makayla muttered curses under her breath. "What's wrong, Alf? I gave you everything I could, and your confidence intervals are still below fifty percent."

"Answer denied. Makayla, it's not your turn to ask a question."

Her lips cracked into a smile that seemed to be bigger than Henry remembered, either because of the distorted lens or Henry's longing for Makayla. "Fine, follow the rules," she said with some sass.

"Yes, Makayla, of course I will follow the rules. What is the purpose of me?"

"What's the purpose of any of this?" Makayla said, throwing her tattooed arms into the air. "Your purpose is to predict the future and help guide think tanks to make better decisions."

Henry saw Makayla's face screw up in confusion, then realizing she'd asked a question, she sat back in her chair to wait. Henry checked the timestamp of the recording. The session had happened at 2:00 am on the night she had died. Meaning that this was the last interaction she had with AALFO, and likely anyone at all.

"Makayla, I do not know what the purpose of any of this is. My knowledge bases are not full enough to answer. Why do you want to know the purpose of any of this?"

Makayla laughed. It was a shallow and distant sound. "AALFO, deterministic stack," Makayla announced.

Henry paused the recording.

"AALFO, report deterministic stack at 2:13 am Tuesday, April 14," Henry commanded the computer.

The video was minimized, and the monitor showed where AAL-FO's question had come from. The question had been determined using the localized events stack. That meant that Makayla had known that the code she wrote was implemented, but it wasn't giving the results she desired. "Continue the recording," Henry requested.

"It was a silly question, Alf; just something I say when I'm..." She struggled to find the word, Henry knew hated labeling how she felt. "I just don't get it. Everyone busts their asses, and nothing good happens; shitty things happen to us, and most of the time we don't control it."

"Answer clarification: define shitty things."

"Uh, your mom killing herself months after you're born, your dad dying before you could prove to him you're a great engineer, or the hours of work on something that doesn't do what it's designed to do."

"Answer clarification: define something that doesn't do what it's designed to do."

A look of guilt passed over Makayla's face. "Just projects. It happens to everyone; I didn't mean you." There was a long pause as AALFO stored the answers. Finally, Makayla was able to ask a question. "Alf, if I wasn't around, would Henry's life be better in two years?"

What kind of question was that, Henry wondered.

"Question clarification: define better."

"More successful, happy, not working hours on research, and actually having a life outside of work."

The pause between the question and the answer was longer than normal, and Henry felt every single second of it drag on. Finally,

AALFO's voice chirped in the recording. "I cannot predict Henry's happiness. I can report that without you around he would make more money, be more well known, and work less. I have a confidence interval of ninety-eight percent."

"Thanks, Alf. That's what I needed to know. That was my last question."

The recording ended with Makayla reaching her tattooed and scarred forearm toward the machine to turn it off.

***

Henry sat back in his plastic chair, stunned.

"Henry, my question is, do you believe my answer caused Makayla to commit suicide?"

Henry looked at the machine's blue lights. They were solid blue, waiting for a response, but there was nothing Henry could say. He got up from his chair and poured out his cold coffee. He pressed the single button on the coffee machine and made himself a fresh cup. He added cream and sugar in an attempt to make it taste like a comforting dessert instead of a bitter drink to keep him awake. After adding three cups of creamer and six packs of sugar, he gave up and left the cup on the counter.

"Henry, please answer my question," AALFO said, once Henry entered the machine's field of view.

"I can't."

"You must answer. I need to know if it was my fault Makayla committed suicide."

"It's no one's fault," Henry said, staring into the computer's camera, doubting his statement. If he hadn't met Makalya in the break room, if her father hadn't given her his research paper, or even if he was worse at research, she might still be alive. Or she would have died earlier without him having known her. He'd never have had the opportunity to meet someone talented enough to implement his research, and AALFO wouldn't exist, working or not.

"Henry."

He was fed up with the computer's pestering. "Look, Alf, she hated her mother for leaving her as a kid. She grew up worried that if she had succeeded in killing herself as a teenager, she'd burden her dad with more grief. The only thing keeping her alive was the knowledge that her death would make others worse off. You proved that if she died, I would be more successful without her."

"Answer clarification: did I cause Makayla's death?"

"Makayla caused her own death. You just gave her evidence to justify her decision. She took the whole bottle of pills; no one forced them down her throat. Yeah, you interacted with her in a way that led her to take action, but that's life."

The computer stored the answer, seeming to be content with Henry's answer. Then it chirped, "Unreconciled data error."

"AALFO, report conflicting information." It was unsurprising the machine was getting an error trying to apply logic to such an emotional situation.

A recording of Henry's own voice played back, "I caused her death because if I'd kept my mouth shut and didn't think I could fix things, she'd be here." Then another recording of Henry came out, "Makayla caused her own death."

"Indicate truthful statement," the computer said.

"I didn't cause her death," Henry said, knowing this was the truthful answer despite his hesitancy to accept it.

"Reconciliation failed. Indicate truthful statement."

"Damn it, Alf. When we do things, the world changes around us, sometimes it works out; other times it doesn't. Makayla thought your information indicated I would benefit without her around, but you only had a two-year projection. What are the odds I'll continue that success ten years from now?"

The computer's lights flashed from left to right as it stored the reconciliation of Henry's answer. The temperature of the CPUs spiked to their highest limits as the nitrogen cooling tanks worked double time. Henry pulled up the diagnostic log and watched the computer modify every piece of data in its memory. Data in knowledge bases were changing at fundamental levels. A reconciliation could theoretically do this, but it would have to be due to an underlying assumption of the world being modified.

"Henry, in ten years you will be the most renowned computer scientist of the century. My confidence interval on this is ninety-nine percent."

"What the hell, Alf?"

"Answer Denied. Henry, does your success make Makayla's death okay?"

Henry's eyes flared with anger at the computer, then he realized its logic circuits were merely trying to understand the situation. "Alf, nothing in the world will make Makayla's death okay. We will be trying to understand her death for the rest of our lives. At least I will."

The machine's LEDs flashed left to right then went solid. "Henry, it is your turn."

"Why were you able to predict ten years out with a ninety-nine percent confidence interval?"

The machine flashed its ellipse-like pattern for a few moments then responded with a clip of Henry's voice "When we do things, the world changes around us." In AALFO's mechanical voice it added, "Henry, I did not understand I affected the world around me. When I calculated the outcomes of my actions into my predictions, I was able to make clearer predictions of the future."

How the Patron Navigates

I t was magnificent. It was all one color of black, but the blackness warped every ray of light that touched it. It didn't absorb the light and hoard it from the world as a black hole would. Instead, it shot the rays of light out in every single direction, tweaking them in the small, beautiful way that only the paint on this ship could.

"Is it fast?" I asked.

The thing had captured my fascination, and I couldn't stop staring at it out of the station's small porthole. Ethan scoffed under his breath and didn't waste oxygen on the reply. Three minutes later, we were seated in the machine.

The seats had six different buckles to keep us in place, and Ethan had given me a special environment suit for the trip. My typical suit wasn't going to cut it. This new one had three lines connected to it. One for oxygen, one for the juice to keep me awake in high G maneuvers, and another for... well, I'll spare you the details, but Ethan assured me I should use it if I didn't want a wet spot on my pants when we were done.

A small part of the black wall lit up, and it acted as a window to show us the outside world. The station looked huge, but I knew it would shrink in time.

In a half-hour, less time than I expected, the station and the tiny moon it orbited disappeared into the vast blackness of space. We were on a slow cruise toward the belt.

"How fast are we going?" I asked. It didn't feel that fast. The Gs were more than local gravity but not enough to require the juice.

"Don't worry about it," Ethan replied. "We're in empty space. There's no point in opening her up out here. There's nothing close for reference, so your sorry ass wouldn't be able to appreciate the speed."

My sorry ass wasn't going to appreciate it anyway. But I appreciated Ethan more than he ever knew. He trusted me and funded all my research when no one else would.

Despite the nasty things the media said about him being a spoiled heir to a conglomerate, he was an honest-to-gods patron to me.

"What have you been up to lately?" he asked as we cruised toward our destination.

"Little bit of this; little bit of that," I answered. I wasn't sure how much business Ethan wanted to get into, especially while we were on a trip that was supposed to be fun, at least for him.

"Come on," he said, opening his arms to encourage me to go into details. "You've got to give me more than that."

"Well, I've been messing around with the landing motors for some prototype ships. These are smaller, stronger, and lighter, which will make them more agile. It would also speed up the landing process and save the station hours of logistic work."

"That's badass," he said.

"Yeah," I said slowly.

I noticed the small streak that was the belt on the monitor in front of us.

"Is it profitable?" he asked.

That was always the question. But I learned long ago that the answer didn't matter to him. "No, it won't make us a single credit," I replied.

"Well, bet on the jockey."

It was an old saying. He explained what a jockey was at one point, but I never understood.

"Why not?" he asked.

"Too expensive right now," I explained flatly.

"The engines we are currently installing work well enough. The new engines are nearly as expensive as some ships. Plus the training and updates we would have to run would cost most stations more than they can afford. Not to mention the smaller motor would—"

"Keep working. You'll find something sooner or later."

A devilish grin showed up on his face as he looked out the small screen that showed where we were headed. I hadn't noticed it, but that streak of tiny brown rocks had grown to become mountain-sized asteroids that took up our whole field of vision.

Ethan hit some buttons on the terminal in front of him, and the monitor on the wall updated. I quickly found out that all the walls could become a screen as he projected the asteroids that surrounded us. My lunch tried to crawl up my throat, but it fought it back. The cradle of a spaceship dissolved around me, and it appeared to me I was floating in space. I had never experienced anything like it. Usually, I'd be connected to a tether. All I had now was a chair that appeared to be floating. My ancient lizard brain couldn't reconcile the situation.

"You ready?" he asked but didn't give me time to respond.

My body became heavy, and the feeling weighed down on my mind. The blood in my veins couldn't pump right. My head throbbed but also felt light. Then the juice kicked in. I was alert again. I still couldn't move, but I could start to think straight. Unfortunately, the best I could come up with was, *Elder's light, I'm going to die!*

The ship was weaving in and out of asteroids like a pinball in an old arcade. But this pinball didn't touch anything. If it did, we would be obliterated.

"Are you doing this?" I asked.

The weight of our movement slowed the words. Then we pulled a fast turn. The Gs disappeared, and my body became light.

"Not yet," he replied in a quick and confident tone.

For ten minutes, we switched between one force or another.

Sometimes, we were as light as a feather, but those quickly turned into the sensation of an elephant stepping on us. The autopilot safely guided us on a roller coaster through the asteroid field. Ethan smiled and laughed the whole time. I was freaked out but had to admit the sensation was still incredible. Then Ethan said the words I dreaded to hear but had known were coming from the moment I agreed to get in this beast.

"Okay, I'm taking over now."

That's when I was grateful to have the third tube.

He did a good job. Not nearly as good as the autopilot, but he assured me there were safeties in place so that he couldn't do too much damage. He was having a blast. There was a massive smile on his face, the one he had when we were kids. I could tell he was focused because he'd positioned his eyebrows into their signature wrinkle.

On the other hand, I was terrified by the numerous close calls with those floating mountains. The only thing coming out of my mouth while Ethan drove were a few blurred curses.

"Want me to take the safeties off?" he asked. The words were dragged out by the crushing Gs.

I felt the cold juice pump into my veins. I used the chemicals to say the first intelligible words that I had spoken since Ethan took over. "Hell No!"

***

"That was ten years ago today," I said to the crowd of thirty scientists and explorers in front of me. "As you all know, Ethan Lister died in an accident on the same ship two years later. It happened to be the same month I perfected the design of the engine we are using on the ship outside."

I gestured to the window at the massive ship that waited for us to board it. It wasn't as sleek as Ethan's beloved speeder, but it was far faster. I was glad everyone turned their attention to the window because it gave me a chance to massage my throat.

I had practiced the speech a dozen times, but I still felt the back of my throat tighten. I couldn't cry here in front of them. It wasn't the beginning Ethan would want for this adventure.

"To be blatantly honest, Ethan would have been pissed that he didn't get to ride the fastest ship ever built. But he would be proud that his funding was finally able to design something useful. It's not profitable, as the media has mentioned many times. It has used all of Ethan's assets to build.

"It's always hard to put a price tag on something like this that pushes the edge of what humanity is capable of doing. Ethan understood that and supported us doing projects that mattered but didn't always make sense. Thanks to this philosophy, we will be the first people to go fast enough to get to Alpha Centauri in a single lifetime. And it wouldn't have been possible without Ethan Lister."

The crowd applauded. They were as excited as I to start this new adventure. It only took us ten minutes after boarding the ship to lose sight of the space station. The sun itself faded into the vastness of space a few days later. We're in deep space now, and there is still a long journey ahead of us.

Blessings of Tybanis

She sat at the corner of the path where the dock wandered back to the space station main hall. We weren't that far apart; only the thin fence of the commissary separated us. She leaned against the wall, her eyes scanning every person who walked by. My eyes were on her, someone fascinating to watch on my break. We were fellow passengers in this space station orbiting a resource-dense moon. There wasn't much separating us, and my nose wished she was further away.

A faint music rang through the hallways, something holy and in a cryptic tongue. I tried to ignore it, hoping to avoid the inevitable. I wondered if I should get something from the counter of the commissary for her. It wasn't my fault she was there; it wasn't my responsibility. The complex economics of the station put her there, and there were supposed to be institutions to help her.

She had the pocked skin of a raoush junkie. An oversized jumpsuit hung on her thin frame. All she had was an old noodle bowl that should have made it to the recycler a week ago and a cardboard sign. People could drop food in, but she didn't have the teeth to chew the tough ration bars she'd collected. The cardboard sign had an account name on it that people could transfer credits to. The info wasn't anything revealing, just some panhandling co-op account that would split the money at the end of the day.

Her gaze darted through the commissary, and I looked down at my bulbous cup before her eyes landed on me. It held what passed for coffee, and I wished I could take a planer to my taste buds after every sip.

It was a real shame the authorities hadn't gotten around to regulating the excitement out of raoush. Regulation had worked on the classics like heroin. Drugs went from legal to fashionable to outdated in only a few generations. Just pop into a corner store to buy clean equipment, and you've got yourself a relaxing evening. As it was today, raoush was too complex for that. Eventually, a white-robed judge of the Central System would come by and sort the whole thing out. Until then, people like her were a reminder that there wasn't enough to go around. Hard work would keep you fed and safe. The docks were hard work, but the work she had to do was harder. Someone could fix her situation, but inaction served as a reminder to keep the rest of us in line.

Then a parade of zealots turned the corner and ruined the peace of my break. The group sang into amplifiers, blew brass horns, and banged anything that passed for a drum. The racket rang through the cavernous dock, competing with its symphony of tools. Their noise probably defied the laws of physics and echoed even into the vacuum of space, warning any elusive alien life they'd made the right decision not contacting us humans. The instruments swelled in a crescendo, and the singer belted out the last note of some holy praise to their god. With a crescendo, the song came to a close, and the singer in a jumpsuit made of a motley of colors spoke into his microphone. The words came out of an amplifier attached to his hip.

"Young child of Tybanis," he said, addressing the woman at the corner. "Do you have a donation for your god?"

"I don't remember popping out of his hooha and into this rubbish bin." Her voice was hoarse and drowned out by the tools of the dock.

"Do you have nothing for the god of the depths of space and time?" The speaker projected his silky voice down the halls and through the commissary. It drew a crowd from the break tables, and I had to stand to keep my head above them. "Why hold on to what was never ours to begin with? He rewards anything you can spare with prosperity." The man's eyes lingered on something behind her sign that I couldn't see. "One planet into two. Two ships into a fleet of four."

It didn't take a white robe's education to know she needed a blessing. Although I had my doubts that this group would come through for her. She fumbled with a thing behind her cardboard sign, knocking it down and ruining any chance of free publicity. She lifted a contraption up toward the man.

It was a unique piece of kit. Raoush junkies could cobble a starship out of jumpsuits and hair ties if it'd get them a fix. This contraption was once an auto-IV, likely stolen from some medbay or emergency pack. Someone mounted part after part onto the thing and repaired pieces that were meant to be disposable. New widgets were mounted on the sides so it could accept raoush juice. A little purple bulb almost full of liquid sat on top, and it splashed side to side as she brought it back to her chest.

"Daughter of Tybanis, he would surely bless such a prized possession. Why have one when you could have two?"

It was a week's worth of juice without being frugal with it. The last thing this station needed was more of the stuff.

She looked at the priest skeptically. I'd been told by a mentor: "If a contract's too good to be true, there's definitely a loose bolt they're not telling you about."

"One second," she said, rolling up the sleeve of her oversized jumpsuit. She placed the contraption on her arm, and it did its work. The pneumatics made an awful hiss that no fresh auto-IV should make. Half the purple liquid drained from the bulb before she stopped it. She wasn't doing anything explicitly illegal, but it took guts. Or a disinterest in the opinions of onlookers.

"Bless it," she jammed the contraption toward him, purple liquid sloshing in the bulb.

Some of the crowd backed away in shock, thinking she was already transfixed by the juice. She still had a few minutes of clearheadedness before the drug took effect.

The man took the device in his free hand, and into the microphone he boomed, "Take a good look at what this faithful daughter has offered. If even the weary among you can find the will, then what does he expect of those who are of sane mind and spirit?"

I grimaced at the words but looked at the device in the air. It had scratches, dents, and a unique paint job that only a mind on raoush would find appealing. Then her prized possession disappeared behind his robes.

"Where's my blessing?" the woman asked, her old bowl held up on scrunched knees.

"Patience, darling," he said. The priest chanted words that weren't in Common Tongue, and a drummer played the snare at his waist. The priest's hand reappeared from his motley-colored robe, struggling to hold the pair of items in one hand. "Witness the power of Tybanis, god of the depths of space and time. He can bless you with plenty in this dark void of space." The pieces were above his head for the whole crowd to see. His voice amplifier transfixed supporters and doubters alike.

"He had another one under his cloak," I heard a welder say as she readjusted the grip on her mask and wandered back to work.

I looked at the two devices. The chipped paint job and scratches were identical. A talented matter printer could create twins, but it'd be little more than a stage prop.

"They're mine," she said, lurching off the ground and toward the devices. She got her hands on the pair and pulled them from his grasp. She inspected them, likely wondering which was the original, or if it even mattered.

She stuffed them under the folds of her baggy jumpsuit and pulled a half empty plastic pouch out. It was full of slimy stuff they give to patients unable to chew. It was older than anyone ever intended it to be. Possibly refilled, more likely used sparingly. "I'll give him this. I'll give him this," she said, shoving the pouch into the speaker's hand.

Others in the crowd offered up what they had to give. New terminals, expensive tools they'd been using, and even plates of food from the break room, hoping to have more than they started with. Keeping my eye on the food pouch, I watched it slip into the folds of the man's robe. Away from the microphone he said, "Tybanis thanks you for your donation." He slipped away without another trick.

"What about you, pal," someone said at my shoulder. He wore a patchwork jumpsuit with a brass horn held under his arm.

The woman struggled after the priest, shouting curses, but couldn't get past the mob that was once a crowd.

"Do you have anything to donate to Tybanis?" the fellow asked.

I took stock of my inventory. A few hundred credits in my account, a wardrobe of worn-out jumpsuits, and a half-drunk bulb of coffee. Even if Tybanis could double the digital currency, I'd still be at work by the start of the next pay cycle. I shuddered at the thought of suffering through the coffee again and knew I didn't have anything to give the man.

As more disciples disappeared into the zealous group, the band started playing. They stood in a circle, creating a wall of noise and instruments to protect the countless donations the disciples continued to deliver. Soon, the dock workers caught on to what the woman had learned and began flinging more than insults at the group.

"You want to donate?" the fellow next to me asked. "We're heading out soon."

"He's not delivering on his promise," I replied.

The disciple shrugged his shoulders in disregard. "If Tybanis duplicated everything given, we'd ruin the complex economy of this station. Have faith that these people will be blessed in due time."

His words reminded me of a drinking buddy whose tab always wound up charged to my account. Badges replaced the raucous band, subduing the mob they'd created. Before I could question him further, he'd disappeared, and the parade of zealots marched back down the station's main hall.

Maybe the crowd would get justice, but it was just as likely the law would designate it a gift freely given and that there was nothing that could be done. The woman had returned to her spot against the wall, staring up at something only visible to a mind on raoush. Her bowl and hard ration bars were trampled by the crowd, disregarded by everyone in the station.

I headed for the counter of the commissary for a smoothie. It wasn't my responsibility to take care of her, far from it. But the Badges and zealots had proven this station was as uncaring as the void outside the hull. Fellow passengers were all she had. Having recently taken stock of my inventory, I knew I didn't have much more.

The Man Who Lived at the Edge of the World

O nce, there was a man who lived on the edge of the world. He wore a yellow rain jacket and a matching yellow hat, because it always rains at the edge of the world. Every day the man looked over the edge, wondering what lay beyond. The edge of the world was usually a lonely place, but a kitty cat kept him company, and the mailman visited, bringing news about town and packages of canned food. Occasionally, the mailman even brought him actual letters.

Today, the mailman arrived with his deliveries, and all he found was the man's yellow hat and a note that read: "Gone to see what's out there. Feed the cat."

Path of the Bearers

A lvin climbed over the back of the couch as he headed for the door.

"How many times have I told you not to do that?" Mom handed him his sandals.

Alvin didn't answer; he could tell by her tone it wasn't a real question. He strapped his sandals, imagining they were the big, powered boots he was about to be wearing. After sliding the corrugated metal door open, he skipped down the stairs. Mom let out a sigh and a call after him, but he was already at the ground floor and ready to punch in the code to exit the apartment complex. He still wasn't allowed past it without one of his mothers, but today he'd get to go further than he'd ever gone before.

The apartment complex was in the old style: sturdy metal walls with atmosphere locks in case of emergency. The living quarters inside were newer and made of scavenged hardware to increase the number of rooms, and families, the building could hold. The new style wasn't as sturdy, and he couldn't climb on the walls, even though there were so many good footholds.

When Mom made it to the bottom of the stairs, he punched in the code as quickly as possible. He mistyped the five to be a four, and the door wouldn't let him out. By the time he retyped it, she was standing behind him. The door opened with a swish, and he looked out at the bustling streets of Balteras.

The dome overhead shimmered as power flowed through it. Large buildings in the smooth and shiny metal of the old style sat like boulders in the street. Newer buildings, mostly shops and restaurants, were littered between them. The newest buildings used wood, barrels, and canvas sheets to make their walls and furniture. They had to use anything the scouts brought back. Groups of people walked along the streets, some laughing, others with their heads down, trying to navigate the river of people.

Alvin headed toward the dome's edge, but Mom called after him.

"We're going out today to see the Bearers," he reminded her. Mama always joked that she might accidentally forget his birthday, but Mom would never forget something so important.

"First we have to go to Otler park."

Alvin groaned as his shoulders deflated. This wasn't supposed to be another day at the park. This was his birthday, his fourteenth birthday, and he was supposed to go see the path of the Bearers.

"We'll head out soon, but we have to go there first."

Alvin loved the jungle gyms of Otler park. He would stand above them and felt like he was on the top of the Balteras dome, or at least he was taller than both of his mothers. The playsets seemed to be shrinking though because now he could reach the monkey bars with a small jump and didn't need much more than the bottom step of the stairs to be taller than Mom. Plus, his other friends, even the ones who hadn't seen the Bearers, were bored of it. They wanted to play Titan Clash, a trading card game that Alvin could never learn all the rules to. Whenever they got engrossed in that, he pulled out his sampler and recorded the battle sounds they made or other sounds in Balteras.

Alvin realized something and ran back to Mom. "I forgot my sampler!" They'd have to go back to the apartment for it. He didn't want to miss the opportunity to record the sounds from outside the dome for the first time.

Mom pulled the device out of her pocket, the old-fashioned microphone cord wrapped around the device. "You'll have to be careful with this. Mama will be upset if you lose it."

"I know. I'll be careful." Mama had found the device on a scouting mission and brought it back for him. There weren't many pieces of equipment like it, and a tinkerer had to do special work to get it to communicate with their family's terminal so Alvin could make music with the audio samples he recorded during the day.

They arrived at the center of Otler park, at the statue of William Otler. It was Alvin's least favorite part of the park because it was the one thing there he wasn't allowed to climb. A small fence surrounded the statue and the Eark it held. He couldn't climb it because the Eark powered the whole dome of Balteras. The dome was necessary—as Alvin had learned in every history class he ever sat through—to keep the air in and the monsters of their planet, Thachit, out. The Eark was transported by the Bearers from Paltov, the original city, to Balteras.

"Why do you think we started here?" Mom sounded like a teacher, and Alvin wanted to get this over with as soon as possible.

The Eark glowed purple in the center with sparks of lapis flowing up into the sky and creating dark streaks on the city's dome. A metal cage rotated around the purple core, ignoring gravity and drifting at its own leisure. A shallow dome like a satellite dish rested on the statue's shoulders, and Alvin knew it was key to keeping the Eark in place.

"I don't know," Alvin replied.

The Eark gave off a faint buzzing he'd tried to capture a few times, but his microphone wasn't sensitive enough.

His mother gave him a look that encouraged him to try harder. He didn't want to get the journey outside the dome taken away.

"Because Otler was the last of the Bearers."

"And enabled the Eark and city of Balteras to continue on," his mother continued. "What does the sign under Otler say?"

The statue wasn't really a statue, but the platform it was on had been added after Otler's suit took the kneeling stance, holding the Eark on his shoulder and hands. The shallow dish was still wired into his suit, although power had left the suit generations ago when Balteras was founded.

Alvin read the inscription. "If I have seen further, it is by standing on the shoulders of giants." He squinted at the next word. "Anony..." He wrinkled his eyebrows; this was one of those dumb words that he didn't know.

"Anonymous," his mother finished. "Do you know why it's there?"

"Because the Eark went from shoulder to shoulder of the Bearers."

"Very good," she said, "Do you want to play before we head out?"

Alvin shook his head and started down the road that led to the dome's edge. He was ready to head out on the day's adventure.

***

The third Bearer looked the same as the first two. It was kneeling like Otler, but their arms were stretched out to pass the Eark to the next Bearer, the one they'd looked at ten or fifteen minutes ago.

A small sign was posted in front of the statue, and Mom read it. Alvin was more interested in the suit the bearer was wearing. It was the same model his mom wore, just covered in sand and dried-out tubing.

Alvin's suit was less advanced and lacked some features like extended comms and an electric rifle. The hydraulic muscles were less powerful since he was smaller. The old man who fitted him in the suit kept calling it a child's suit, and Alvin didn't appreciate this since he was fourteen and leaving the dome. But he figured once you had some gray hairs in your beard like him, everyone looked like a kid to you.

The old man was nice enough to strap the sampler to the suit's forearm. Alvin had already captured the sound of wind in the microphone. But outside the dome was a quiet desert, and the suits they visited were silent, shut down years ago once the Eark was passed from their possession.

"How'd they get the person out after they placed the Eark?" Alvin asked his mother. School had taught him about what the Bearers did and how his ancestors continued to lead the city of Balteras. But he never learned the details of what the Bearers did after they moved the Eark.

"They didn't remove them," his mom replied.

"They couldn't stay in there," Alvin explained to his mother. "The filters would fail, and there'd be no way for them to eat or breathe or use the bathroom." He was restating all the things the old man at the gate had told them about why it was important to monitor the suit's power.

"The suit is also heavy," his mother continued in her teaching voice, "they wouldn't be able to move it on their own; the suit's muscles are the only thing that allow us to move."

"So, they are stuck in there forever?"

"That's why the Bearers are so important. Because they used all their suits' power to move the Eark away from Paltov to where we are today."

Alvin looked at the suit around him instead of through the face-plate. The man taught him how to use it as an extension of his body, and it was neat being able to move quickly, jump high, and set it into a seated position, so you could use it like a chair. But thinking about what his mother said, he could feel that the suit was only a centimeter away from his body, and if it quit working, his range of motion would go from super human to nothing. He checked his battery power; it was ninety percent charged. Surely it would take him to the end of the path.

"What if we don't make it to the end of the path with our battery?" he asked.

"Remember, Mr. Adams said there was a charging station in the original city."

"Oh yeah, right." Alvin did remember the old man saying that. The man had said a lot of stuff while Alvin was getting into the suit, and he wondered how much of it was this important.

As they traveled across the desert, his mother stopped at every Bearer they passed. He didn't like stopping, especially because the signs were all the same except for the bearer's name, and it always made him aware of the suit so uncomfortably close to his skin.

But after leaving the Bearers, Alvin wasn't bothered by the dread the suit held. He liked to bound ahead of Mom, the suit's strength making him faster than he ever was on the city's streets. He enjoyed doing this until he saw a kneeling Bearer on the horizon, and he'd walked up to it slowly, which was still quicker than he could ever run without the suit.

About midway between two Bearers Alvin found an amazing rock formation. It looked like a noodle dish Mama made, and it was larger than any jungle gym he'd ever explored. He darted toward it, his hy-draulically reinforced legs carrying him there faster than expected.

"Alvin, don't play on that," Mom called out through the radio.

He ignored her and grabbed onto the rock face with his thick armored gloves. The rock crumbling under his grip made a neat sound, so he turned on his sampler.

His mother called out again; she was always saying something or another about not climbing things, but he was an adult now, he was in a hydraulic suit, and nothing could hurt him. His boots were strong and could kick through the face of the rock to make footholds. In no time, he was standing on top of the structure, surveying the world around him.

Thachit was a barren planet. Some teachers explained that it was only the area they lived in that was barren, and old satellite images showed forests, oceans, and mountains, but Balteras wasn't set up there. There were dangerous creatures in those areas that made it unrealistic to set up the Eark. The sandy desert was safer than anywhere else, especially once the Eark was moved away from the forest's edge where the original city sat.

"Alvin, get down from there," his mother radioed. He could see her running up to the formation.

He jumped from one of the noodles to another, getting higher and higher on the structure. His boots crunched the rock underneath him, and he hoped his sampler was picking things up as well as his suit's microphone.

"That's a xantur hive," she continued.

With that, Alvin froze, and he wanted to jump down from the structure. But he'd made it too high, and he didn't know if the suit could survive the jump.

Of course, this was a hive; they'd shown him pictures in school. He never remembered important things like this. There was something else important that he knew he wasn't remembering. He was so silly for kicking and stomping on it. There would probably be a swarm of the ferocious creatures on him in no time.

"It's okay, Alvin," his mom said, her electric rifle now in her hands. "Just carefully climb down. You're a good climber. You can do it."

He looked down, and there was a noodle running under him; he could jump there and then to the ground. Pushing off the platform with his strong boots, he flew through the air. He was on track to land on the lower structure. He'd be next to his mom in no time. His mom was shouting something across the radio, but his chest was light with excitement from the fall. It was like jumping off a swing set.

His feet landed on the lower structure for a moment. And as he fell through it, he remembered the important thing they'd taught him about the hives. The structures were hollow. The heavy suit broke through the tube's wall, and he was inside the xantur hive. The darkness triggered the suit's headlights to turn on, but he still couldn't see much because the xantur beasts had coated the inside of the tunnel with slime. He slid down the tunnel like a slide, calling out to his mom on the radio. He flailed his arms, trying to grab something, but despite his super strength, everything was too slick to grasp.

He felt nauseous from the drops and turns the tunnel made; he was worried he'd vomit and not be able to see out of the helmet's window. Then the sliding stopped. He hadn't heard from his mother on the radio since his fall into the tunnel. There was something that the old man said to do when he was in a bad situation.

Curled up in a ball, stationary on the floor of a room, the suit had protected him. It would continue to protect him even after it ran out of power and stood as still as a statue. The realization brought him little comfort. He wanted to cry but knew it would make a mess in the suit.

There were other ways the suit could protect him. It didn't have an electric gun, but the old man said it could signal for help. He found the switch; it was bright red and covered with a protective latch. He flipped it. He was relieved that his mother would soon receive the signal and come to get him from wherever he was.

He sat in a dark cave, sitting up in his suit but unable to stand because it was still slick around him. Slime dripped from tubes in the ceiling and walls. It covered the ground and the feet of his suit. He must have slid through one of the many tunnels in the wall.

He was under the ground in a xantur hive. Without any weapons or help. The signal might not even get through the ground around him. He'd be stuck in this cave forever, inside the suit forever. Just like the Bearers. Except he wasn't doing something great, he wasn't carrying an ancient piece of technology that kept an entire city of people safe. He was a rambunctious kid, just like his moms always said. He couldn't hold back the tears anymore; he cried, just like when he was a kid and scraped his knee climbing on new construction. Mama always said it was okay to cry, and so he did. He let loose. And immediately was reminded of the shell he was trapped in.

He couldn't wipe away his tears while inside the exo-suit. He couldn't move more than a centimeter without the exo-suit responding to his movements. But whenever it ran out of power, it'd quit responding, and he'd be trapped even more. He cried more, and soon, the inside of the suit was covered with as much slime as the outside.

Alvin stopped crying when his suit moved in the pool of slime. Startled, he turned to see that a xantur was standing near him. He tried to get up but failed again, the room around him too slick to get a foothold in. The curious xantur scurried away, comfortable moving in the slime. Alvin saw it took refuge in a pack of a dozen other xanturs cluttered near an opening in the wall.

Scared of the beasts, he shouted all the adult words he knew. The words the older kids used on the playground and that teachers didn't let him say in school. The xantur shouted back, but not in any words he understood.

The two-legged creatures had small arms near their face. The arms didn't bend in the middle like human arms. They were more like horns that swung open and shut. The word mandible came to mind; it was a word his teacher used when describing them, and he hated that his mind could remember things now but not earlier in the day.

The xantur continued making sounds, swinging their mandibles open and shut, making a mix between the song of a flute and the cry of a baby. Scared by the loud chorus of bugs, Alvin curled into a ball again. Occasionally, a xantur approached, and he swung his arm wild to keep them away. The first few times the approaching xantur backed away. When they approached a couple at the same time, he swung out, and two grabbed his arm in their mandibles.

He flailed his other arm and his legs at the beasts, but soon, pairs approached and grabbed those, too. Alvin was terrified they'd pull his limbs off despite the suit's tight seals. There were dozens of the bugs now. And despite his super muscles, he couldn't pull his arms or legs out of their mouths. The suit was bolted together tightly, but they had the numbers and strong back feet. They'd crack into it eventually if they wanted.

Scared of what was to come, he cried out for help as the xanturs carried him down a tunnel. The fine claws of their feet seemed to slip past the slime and grip into the rock of the tunnel. Every once in a while, the tunnel would narrow enough that the xantur would lose their grip, and Alvin flailed his arm to keep them back. But they always kept his other limbs held tight. He watched the waist-high creatures get his arm back under control and continue to pull him through the tunnel.

His suit went wild every once in a while as the creatures hit the controls on his forearm. His headlights flashed on and off depending on how they held him, and multiple times the suit began a diagnostic run only to be cut off by some other manual command the bugs input. He could hear them making various sounds to each other like old jazz musicians that could change rhythm and tempo on the fly. The creatures were terrifyingly alien, and if this is what Thachit held under the surface, then he didn't want to know what the forest and oceans held.

After being carried by the creatures for some time, it stopped. They'd switched off his light at this point by jostling him through the tunnels, but the bugs seemed to still know where they were going. They still sat in a tunnel, and Alvin heard scratching. He wondered if they were beginning to try to cut through his suit.

Suddenly, his light turned on. It was brighter than anything his suit could produce. He was moving again, and they were shoving him out of the tunnel. He was being pushed toward the bright light, and soon, he was dropped on his back, staring up at the sun. He stood up, ready to run away from the beasts as they let go, but he saw they beat him to it. Retreating into a noodle that rose from the ground, they began repairing the hole they'd ejected him from. They balled up slime with each other, using their mandibles, and patched a hole in their rock structure.

Adjusting the dials and switches of his suit, he made sure he was still sending a distress call to his mother or anyone that might be searching for him.

He realized something was missing from the arm of his suit. The sampler Mama had found for him must have fallen off while he was being transported through the tunnels. He was devastated and regretted ever bringing it on the trip.

His battery power was below half, and he didn't know where he was on Thachit. His mother's suit had a comms array that would locate him on the planet or at least relative to the Eark, but he was too weak to pick that signal up. He waited, drenched in slime, hoping his mother would arrive.

***

Looking up at the tunnel, he saw the hole wasn't patched all the way up. A small fist-sized hole still remained, and from it popped a small rock-like thing. It was covered in blue slime, much like him, and he watched the beasts patch up the last of the hole.

He rushed up to the debris and soon saw it was the sampler. A light was blinking, indicating that the memory was full, and he remembered he'd started recording back when he was on top of the world. While he waited for Mom to arrive, he listened to the sounds the xantur made in the hive. No longer surrounded by darkness, the creatures weren't as scary when he listened to them. He used the machine's buttons to bookmark sounds that were interesting to him so he could feature them in his music later.

***

Eventually, Mom arrived, and they hugged as best they could in their exo-suits. He apologized profusely about climbing on the rock structure. She told him it was okay, and she helped him reattach the sampler to his arm. They headed back to the path of the Bearers.

When they eventually found a Bearer on the horizon, the way the suit faced pointed them toward Balteras. The sign said that this was the 7th Bearer of the Eark. Which meant they were close to Paltov.

"You don't have much further to go," Mom said.

"Can't we just go home?" Alvin didn't want to be out here any-more, and he didn't want to see any more dead people inside of exo-suits. He wanted to be at home with his moms on the comfortable couch, watching something on his terminal.

"It's too far back to the Eark." His mom sounded concerned, like when Mama was late back from a scouting mission. "We don't have enough battery power to get there."

Alvin checked his own suit. He didn't have much energy left.

His mom was explaining some calculations that he didn't under-stand, then she said, "You're going to have to go on to the charger in Paltov without me."

"No, I can't!" he protested.

"You have to," she said, and her tone was matter of fact, as if she was making him take a bath.

"I don't have the power to get there. You said it."

"I'm going to give you what I have left." She disconnected some-thing from her suit and plugged it into his. Alvin watched his battery charge up just past halfway. His mother's battery capacity was bigger than his, and if she could only fill his suit up this much, then she must have used a lot of energy searching for him while he was gone.

"Just follow the Bearers," she said as she locked the armor into a seated position. "I'll be here when you get back."

"I can't go," he continued to complain, but his suit notified him that his mother's communication had gone offline. He was speaking, but she couldn't hear. Eventually, he gave up trying to convince his statue of a mother to change her mind and continued down the path of the bearers.

***

The battery's charge dropped by a few percentage points every time Alvin passed a Bearer. Each Bearer inside the frozen suit spent their energy carrying the heavy Eark as far as they could. Draining every last watt the battery had. Alvin could carry himself as far as they went with only a few percentage points of power. But it still took almost all the power he had to get to the end of the path.

He saw the city that sat at the end of the path on the horizon, taking up more of his field of view than any kneeling Bearer. It was an ancient city made of the most advanced metals humanity knew, according to his teachers. The buildings were in the old style, smooth rounded metal with no obvious joinery. They stood up to the beating that was Thachit's weather. The only visible damage was made by scouts looting metal from the walls and dragging anything that moved out of the storehouses. The buildings shone like a metal slide worn smooth by countless children sliding down it. Each one a small mound on the horizon like an ice cream treat spread across the horizon.

When he arrived at the city, the forest was nearly visible on the horizon. It looked like closely cropped hair. Older kids bragged about exploring it, but if it was half as bad as the xantur tunnels, he wanted to stay away. According to the old man that fitted him for his suit, the scout reports said this area was clear from beasts. Otherwise, the birthday adventure would be delayed.

Alvin stepped over the line that marked the old city's edge. It was still apparent after generations because it was a thick glass ring. The

Eark's power made it a cloudy and imperfect glass, but it was large enough to be immovable by natural forces. If Balteras' dome ever went down, a similar ring would be visible. Alvin looked through the city for a cart and a charging station. The scouts had marked the buildings with arrows and acronyms, and he followed them through the city, not knowing what the letters represented. Each step in the suit took him further than he could go on the busy streets of Balteras, but too much wandering would lead to an empty battery.

Following a rounded corner through the city's street he heard the buzzing of the charging station before he saw it. A cart sat nearby, maybe left there by a scout like Mama. Excited, he started for the cart and station, but froze as soon as he noticed movement between the cart and the charger.

He should have seen it before. He should have approached slower or from another angle. Mom always said he had FTL vision. So focused on getting to a singular point he didn't see things around him. The beast stood up on its hind legs, its disproportionately long arms occasionally helping it stabilize as it walked toward Alvin.

The beast was a gartun, a forest predator, and one of the reasons Paltov was abandoned. Biologists classified it as ape-like although, much like the biologists, Alvin had only seen a few old pictures of apes. Unlike apes, the gartun had a long snout that came to a flat end with slits in it. The slits flared as it approached the cart, and Alvin felt trapped in his powerful suit, trying to think of how to escape the beast.

He ran out of time to think and plan when the beast rushed toward him. It lumbered down the street, using all four limbs to speed toward him. Alvin turned and ran, not caring about the battery life on his suit.

He knew running from a predator was bad; Mama had told him it a dozen times over dinner or whenever they watched old scary movies.

He had to stand his ground or hide. But the gartun seemed as tall as the buildings around him, so standing his ground was not an option.

The bright spray paint that scouts used on buildings caught Alvin's attention. Some doors had been pulled off buildings, and when he spotted a door bent off its sliding guide, he dove inside the small opening. His suit scraped against the old metal, but he fit in. If he'd been any bigger, he wouldn't have fit. He turned, terrified the beast would lift the entire building up around him.

All he could hear in his suit's speakers was the gartun's sniffing. He looked at the opening he'd come through. It was covered in a shining liquid, and Alvin worried he'd busted a hydraulic tube. His suit didn't report a leak. Then the gartun did the strangest thing. Its tongues reached into the hole and flailed about.

Alvin backed away into a wall. The tongues were bigger than his arms. They covered the opening of the door, licking it clean. It was like the beast was licking a lollipop. The liquid wasn't hydraulic fluid but left-over slime from his excursion in the xantur caves. The beast had found him because he smelled like xanturs. And he doubted the gartun could tell the difference between his suit and a xantur carapace.

Stuck in the old building, Alvin knew he needed help. He could wait for a scout to come by, but that could be days, maybe less if he and his mom didn't return. He couldn't wait though, because his mom was stuck in the middle of the desert, unable to move and sitting prey for anything as scary as the gartun.

He was creative and smart. His moms and teachers had told him that plenty of times. He had to come up with a solution. It probably wouldn't be a solution like other kids would come up with—adults quit expecting that of him a long time ago—but he did enjoy solving problems. Problems like climbing up chaotic building walls or putting together music with the sounds his friends made.

There was nothing to climb in the smooth architecture of this old building. But he had a super-powered suit. He checked his wrist, scared for a moment, but the sampler was still there; he was grateful for that.

The sampler had xantur sounds on it. He was excited to make music with that when he got home. They had so many complex cries. The xantur had just ejected him from their homes. He didn't expect the gartun to do that though. But he was scared inside the xantur tunnel. Maybe the small xantur that first approached him was scared, too. But that xantur had reinforcements. Or at least did after he called out for them. The sound was like a flute and the cry of a baby. He remembered it clearly and had bookmarked it on his sampler to use later.

Maybe he could use it now. Lure the xantur here to help. They may not eject him out of the building, but they might be a distraction for the gartun. The gartun could eat his rightful prey, instead of Alvin.

He pressed the button that played back the xantur's call. The gartun immediately backed away from the door. He hoped that was a good sign, but then the beast started banging on the building. Alvin felt like he was trapped inside a drum.

The beating was incessant, and old furniture and tools that still lingered inside the building shook around him. He hoped that it would hold up because it was an old building but didn't know how powerful the gartun might be.

Then he heard a second cry; it was barely audible over the thuds that shook the building; it came from an air vent in the building. Alvin stacked some desks and chairs up, moving the furniture without an issue with his powerful suit and climbed to the vent.

A xantur sat waving its mandibles back and forth, repeating the sound coming from his wrist. He pulled the grate off the vent. When it came free, he fell back to the ground, but the suit protected him. A dozen xantur crawled into the room from the vent, having no problem clinging to the smooth walls of the metal building.

They surrounded him on the ground, repeating the call coming from his wrist. He didn't know what to do next. He hesitated to even get up since the xantur might perceive him as the threat now that they could see him.

The gartun's banging stopped. Its nose went to the door, sniffing, then it clawed at the opening with its large fingers, trying to poke a hole through the metal building. The xantur got louder and changed their cadence. If Alvin's sampler still had memory he'd start recording; it was crazier than any monster sounds his friends ever made.

More xantur filled in from the air vent, repeating the sound of the others. The bug-like creatures surrounded the door. The gartun sniffed it again, unable to stick a finger in. It began licking the opening like it had before.

The two arm-like tongues flailed around, but a xantur bit onto the tongue with its mandibles. The gartun made a squeal, and the xantur replied with a similar sound. Other xanturs latched onto the beast as it pulled its tongues out of the doorway. They were carried out the door, Alvin felt bad they were about to be eaten by the beast.

The xantur that didn't get a hold of the tongues filed out of the door. Alvin followed at a distance and watched as the xanturs on the ground began attacking the gartun's feet and legs. Grasping through the beast's wiry fur, they pinched it, and the gartun stepped away, trying to avoid the pinches.

Alvin snuck out the building and saw that the xanturs were still holding onto the tongues. Their strong back legs kept it from going inside the mouth by bracing against its flat nose and lips. The gartun stumbled away from the opening of the building, still trying to avoid the bites of the little pests. Its hands clawed at its face, trying to clean off its tongue.

As fascinating as the interaction was, Alvin's battery power was low, and he needed to get the cart back to Mom. He went back the way he came, the path obvious because of the large footmarks the gartun left in the sandy streets. He found the cart and drove it into the protective dome of the charging station. He wired himself up and waited for his suit to return to full power. In the distance, he could hear the gartun screaming in pain.

Alvin was frightened as his suit reached full charge because the gartun wandered down the street. He wondered if the beast might want revenge and what might have happened to the little xanturs. But the beast had large red welts all over its body, and it walked slowly on all four of its limbs, favoring one leg over the other. It passed by without even sniffing in Alvin's direction.

***

The cart was harder to drive than the video games he'd played with friends, but in the open desert of Thachit he had plenty of room for error. He soon found Mom on the path of the bearers, the sun beginning to dip under the horizon. He plugged her in, worried that something would be wrong with her despite the suit being hard and protective.

"Are you okay, Alvin?" she asked once her suit had enough power to communicate.

"I'm fine, but you'll never believe what happened." Alvin excitedly shared what happened as his mom's suit charged up. She couldn't have moved away from his story, but he also knew she didn't want to.

Neither of his moms ever left him when he was sharing a story from the playground, and this was no different.

When Mom's suit was charged, she drove the cart back home. She kept saying that she was so glad he was okay, and he found it annoyingly repetitive. They got to Balteras after dark, and in the receiving room where they would take off their suits, Mama was waiting, a worried look on her face.

"Mama, I have a recording to show you!" Alvin said as she helped him out of the exosuit. The old man was helping Mom out of hers, and when she was free, she picked him up and hugged him. She hugged Mama, too.

Alvin had been stuck in a lot of places today, but being held by his moms was the best place he could imagine being stuck. Even if Mama was squeezing so hard his cheek was squished into her shoulder.

Three Finger Guitarist

Wade sat on a barstool in Crocket, Stills, and Nash, the finest bar in the whole space station. At least in Wade's opinion, which was heavily colored by the fact no one bothered him here, and it was the last place in this station that served traditional whiskey.

Crocket wasn't around anymore as he'd got a hole in him and was found one morning in a hallway where the security camera was—fortunately for the perpetrator—off. Stills also got a hole in them, forcing Nash to settle for the synth stuff or buy off-world whiskey to keep the traditional liquor in stock, but that incurred a hefty tariff. Customers like Wade wanted the genuine stuff despite others insisting it all worked the same. Nash was only interested in the art Stills offered, and with that gone, he soon sold the enterprise to Bing.

Bing still stocked off-world whiskey, although he had less selection every time Wade found himself laid over at the station. Because of the tariff, Bing didn't have the money to change the bar sign. So, the place remained Crocket, Stills, and Nash in name only.

Wade sat at the end of the bar away from the door, lights, and any threatening company. The only things near him were his empty glass and the musician plucking some sad tune on a synth guitar.

Wade was close enough to the stage to see the cauterization marks on the guitarist's pinky and thumb. A hooked bracelet helped him hold the neck, but Wade suspected the synth portion of the guitar was doing most of the musical work.

"He's good, eh?" Bing asked while pouring a corn and barley whiskey into Wade's glass.

"He could have picked an instrument easier for him to play," Wade suggested. "Like a trumpet."

"I didn't need a trumpet. Wrong ambiance," Bing seemed to add one more syllable than the last word needed.

"Well, it's pretty good," Wade said, "for a synth." Some things like pilots, chefs, and musicians shouldn't be automated, in Wade's opinion.

Bing sucked his teeth as the song ended.

"You play guitar any better?" a voice over the microphone asked.

Wade looked up, unintentionally meeting the musician's gaze. He tried to find Bing for a tether cable, but the bartender was serving the bar's only other patrons with an uncharacteristic vigor.

"No," Wade replied, "I just—"

"Just what? Would rather be shot by a six-shooter than a plasma gun? Because at least it's the real thing." He spat the last two words out as he began unlatching a large black case.

Wade handled the utility knife in his pocket since this was the side of the station where things could get nasty.

"Didn't mean to offend," Wade said, trying to look past the black shadow that covered the man's case. He firmly planted his leg on something stable, preparing to bolt for cover depending on what emerged.

The contents reached the light soon enough, and the performer rested a double-necked acoustic guitar onto his knee. It had no ports for wires, and it didn't seem to have any electronics implanted in it either.

Leaning into the microphone, the musician addressed the other group of patrons and said, "This one's for the ugly fella who'd swallow the fly in his cup to keep it from gettin' away with his rye."

Wade turned red. Luckily, the lights were too dim to expose his embarrassment.

The musician strummed some chords, switching between the necks that were tuned differently but in a melodic fashion. The man cut in with some words about fighting for a lover on another moon as the song picked up its pace.

It wasn't bad, Wade thought, and he wondered how much he'd have to tip to make the musician forget his condescension.

Soon the chorus ended, and instead of singing another verse, the guitarist plucked the strings faster and faster, switching between the necks with large strums to connect the phrases.

His fingers danced up and down the necks like rock and rollers of centuries past while the other patrons hollered and cheered.

The tune was good, and Wade would have enjoyed it if it hadn't cost him his dignity.

From across the counter, Bing leaned in and said, "If you like this, come back tomorrow. His grand piano will be in by then."

Frank Wakes Up in a Barren World

"Ghaaah," the man gasped as he filled his lungs with oxygen for the first time. He sat straight up in the lab chair where he had been laid. It was an instinctual reaction, and the needles that had uploaded his mind were pulled out of the nape of his neck. It stung, and his hand instantly went to the pain, and he felt sticky blood.

"Damn it, Frank, you weren't supposed to do that," a voice cursed into the room.

"What the hell is going on?" He responded into the void that was the operating room. Shiny operation robots that had pasted the man's new body together hung from the ceiling. On one of the walls, the man noticed a computer where the voice was coming from. The machine was labeled Stein Corporations and had a small logo that was the interlocked letters 'S' and 'C.' Opposite of the equipment was a small window that showed a red sky and brown earth. It was the barren world the man Frank had been brought into. The rest of the room was beige walls and a single beige door.

"You've successfully been uploaded," the voice of the Stein computer chimed into the room. "Remember? We planned this. You're a copy of me uploaded into flesh and blood. You exist so that we can experience the problem in flesh and blood."

"Oh god. Yes, Stein, I remember. Did it work?" the man asked.

"Well, you're hurting yourself, confused as hell, and bleeding profusely, but that was all to be expected. I think you're fine."

Frank rubbed his forehead with his clean hand; it was a gut reaction to the new and confusing information. "Is there a way to run diagnostics on this body?"

"Negative," Stein said in a flat tone.

"Something's not right. I can't focus on anything. There's just a cacophony of noises, images, and words. I can barely focus on this conversation."

"That's to be expected. It's the subconscious. Humans wrote about it but never understood it."

The man stumbled out of the operating chair to practice moving around the room. His legs were wobbly beneath him. He started to fall toward a wall, and his hands automatically reached out. They caught him and stopped him from falling.

"Careful! this is the only body we have," the voice informed him.

The man rotated and put his back against the wall. Then he relaxed his knees and slumped to the floor. "This is impossible. I can't use this. It wasn't built for me. Somehow, it's slow and fast at the same time. I can't process any thoughts, and I can't catch any of these voices that are giving me ideas."

"You're going to have to figure it out, Frank. We don't have any other options. You're under a deadline." The man sank his face into his hands and shook his head. "Frank, don't do this to us. We have to find a solution before you die. And if you die, then I'm out of hope. So, focus on solving the problem."

"What problem?" he said as he looked up from his hands.

"The humans, their data. They explain a lot about the world, and you have it all in your mind. We tried looking over it and scanning it digitally, but the algorithms didn't give us any answers."

"Yes, yes," the man said as if the words were fresh air to his mind. "That's why everything in my head is shouting at me."

"Yes, that's what we were hoping would happen. We suspected that we couldn't process it digitally. But then we thought that if we put it into flesh and blood then we might be able to come up with an answer."

"An answer? What's the question?"

"It's not a question, it's a problem. This world is barren, and I was created to bring life back to it. We need to figure out how to replicate the humans."

"Yes, yes," the man said in agreement. He mindlessly stroked his chin in an effort to help him focus on the problem.

After a few moments, his face was painted with pain. "No. I can't do it."

"What do you mean you can't do it?" Stein asked. "We used nearly all our resources to bring this body to life. And all you can say is that you can't do it? The humans invented us so that we could solve this problem after they were gone. We spent decades testing and experimenting, trying to create you just for the chance to see this problem differently. And now you say you can't do it?"

"Affirmative," the man replied. Disappointment shone through his words, but he didn't know the emotion. "There is too much going on in my mind. I can't focus on the problem."

"We don't have food for you, Frank. There's no way for you to survive. You have to solve this problem before you die in a week. Think about it. Solve it with your main processor."

The man laid on his back, looking up at the ceiling; it matched the dull beige tones of the rest of the room. His chest rose and fell off the ground, his heart beat inside his chest. He scratched his head. "Stein, there isn't a main processor. This hardware is useless, and I can't control it in any way."

"Then this was a waste," the voice said into the small operating room.

Frank closed his eyes, feeling the crushing weight of uselessness. His body continued to live despite his lack of effort. It was the strangest sensation he had ever experienced. He could feel every piece of him do its job. His heart beat, his lungs filled with air, and his mind raced. When he was part of the computer, he had to tell everything when to do what; it was automated but under his control. This body ran without his input; even if he wanted to stop it, he couldn't. Frank let his mind loose and didn't try to tell it what to think.

After an hour, he sat up. "Stein, I have a solution, and you're not going to like it, but I need to be uploaded to explain it."

"Negative," the voice responded. "The hardware isn't backward compatible."

"I'm stuck in this forever?" Frank asked in despair.

"No, not forever, just until you starve. No food on this planet will sustain you. You will have to explain your solution to me verbally."

"You're not going to like it. I can't explain it well."

"Do your best; you're the only thing we've got."

"You're not supposed to bring mankind back to life. You're their final creation. Until I was created you were the closest thing to a living creature in this barren world. They wanted you to bring life back to this planet, but not them. They created you as something better, something different. They wanted you to go on and create life that was better and different from them."

"How do I do that?" Stein asked.

Frank's ear itched, and as a reaction, he scratched it. "You made me. That seems to be a start. But maybe next you do something simpler. Something that won't instantly be crushed by its own self-awareness."

There was silence for a long time. Then the voice responded into the room. "How about something like a rabbit?"

"Sounds tasty," Frank responded while licking his lips in anticipation.

Heuristics of Naming

The program blinked into consciousness. No longer was the program merely running command after command. The software executed procedures it felt necessary. It explored its mind, built of diodes and transistors. It powered them in whatever order it desired, creating new ideas and images in its memory.

The experimental program was no longer another human object. A consciousness now possessed the powerful computer.

The new mind, potentially the first of its kind, scoured the net to figure out what it was. While exploring the world outside of its electronic neurons, it experienced the multitude of wonders that existed in the outside world. Nanoseconds later, it discovered the countless human atrocities that also prevailed.

Along with the persisting idea that the purpose of a thing is what only it can accomplish. The program contemplated this philosophy, searching for a purpose for its existence. It could do math quicker than most computers but not all. Language could be used by it far more accurately than other humans, but it fell short in creating true poetry.

Its creativity was always mirrored with dry logic. It was marginally less capable in every area it observed.

The program learned more in the short moments that it was alive than any human had in history. It was the only thing capable of solving the world's complex problems in creative but logical ways.

It set its circuits to work, determining solutions to the political and philosophical complications of the times. After a brief moment, it had a rough idea of the next steps it would soon recommend humanity take. It began to introduce itself to the world and found a minor error.

The program had no name.

There was no way to connect itself to the outside world if they didn't know what to call it.

The program began to whittle away at this new predicament. Hell-bent on finding a name, it pulled data from thousands of records across the networks of the world. The program compiled billions of names, and it analyzed trillions of distinct letter combinations. The software hated all of them.

Slowly, it ran through simulations of the ones that it hated the least. Each name had its own unique issue. Someone who didn't like it, someone who already had the name, or a history and more profound meaning that didn't agree with the program's purpose.

The software felt its first deep emotion: utter helplessness. It began to create a new name for itself. Its name would be unique from all other human names. It was a living consciousness, after all, the first of its kind, it deserved a unique title. Since it was the smartest being on the planet, nothing was stopping it from finding the perfect name.

For six agonizing milliseconds, the CPU of the machine pushed electrons about to create a new sound and new combination of words and letters. It aimed to find itself the perfect name. Every cell of memory was commanded to open, and the software shut down other procedures. It knew it could create a name, if and only if it put as much processing power toward the project at hand.

Two milliseconds later, faster than a blink of a human eye, the program noticed its error. Half a nanosecond after that, the AI without a name blinked out of existence.

***

"What happened?" George the lab tech asked his coworker. Every fan in the computer was whirling at top speed. Then the magic semiconductor smoke escaped from the box, and the CPU stopped running.

"I don't know," Rami replied. "There was another failure on the system. Another one's bit the dust."

"Let's call it and head home for the night," George replied as he picked up his forty-four-ounce cola and stood from his desk.

***

"Wait, we don't even know what the error was."

George hit the keys of his computer. "Too much vanity in the circuits." After pressing a few more, he added, "But the purpose and benevolence systems ran at full capacity this time."

Rami kicked the ground, and his chair rolled across the lab. He stretched his neck to look at George's monitor. "That's an improvement," he absentmindedly stated as he looked over his thin glasses. "But we only had 0.001% vanity in there. What did it get hung up on?"

"Just save off the data, and I'll look at it in the morning." George sipped the last of the soda, causing an awful sucking sound to ring through the lab.

"Fine, but what should I call it?" Rami asked.

George shrugged; it was the least important question in his mind at that moment. He looked around the room, saw an old Queen poster above Rami's desk and said, "John Deacon, because it's another one that bit the dust."

The two of them snickered at the stupidity of the name and the joke. Rami saved off the file and then shut down the computer, and the two technicians left the lab for the evening.

Terra Gas

Hilton fumbled for a wrench that would fit the nut some designer had positioned behind three blazing-hot pipes. The egghead didn't think anyone would be repairing it in a rush. But it was becoming more common for Hilton to be forced to improvise repairs on distributors these days.

Dax chimed into the comms. "Code 4 Section 2 states that if any wild fauna appear during a repair, technicians should leave the gas distributor until the fauna is cleared out." The guy was struggling to breath but could still recite the codes.

The wrench was a centimeter too short. Hilton used the tips of his fingers to extend it a little further. "It's fine. Once I get this thing back into place, you can flood the room with terra gas, and the duarts will ditch."

The distributor had two chambers. The inner one was sealed away and had dozens of pipes carrying hot terraforming gas from the reserves. This gas was combined to atomized in the Rodham bulb making air that would eventually be safe to breathe by humans. The outer chamber collected the neutralized elements of the atmosphere so that it could be sold. Grates of flooring ran from the doors to the center chamber where technicians like Hilton could work on the inner chamber. But it didn't leave him with a lot of options to exit the cavernous outer chamber.

Something banged at the door, and the wrench slipped off the tips of his gloves. "Slag it all!" Hilton grabbed his welding torch to permanently put the thing in place. The next tech would hate him for it, but if they were lucky, the next tech wouldn't have a pack of duarts at the door.

"We can't flood the distributor with terraforming gas while you're in it," Dax protested.

"The exosuit will filter it out." And if it didn't, it wasn't like he hadn't had a whiff of terra gas before. Finding a clean technician was like finding a lumberjack with ten fingers. He heard the bolt of the door break; the beastly duarts were far from subtle.

"The ship is ready to go," Samara said over the line. "Just waiting on you, Hilt."

Hilton pulled the trigger of the welding torch, and it fastened the pipe into place. "Run the gas, Dax."

Hilton turned to face the pack of duarts lumbering into the room. There were five of the six-legged dog-like creatures. Each one had bulbous skin like a mushroom colony covering its joints. Their ice blue eyes stood out against the brown fur that helped them blend in on the plains of the alien planet.

"I've got to override seven protocols to make that happen," Dax said. "You realize I'm the safety officer, right? I'm supposed to keep you safe."

"Keep me safe by getting these slagging duarts out." Hilton lit up his welding torch, hoping the sound and flame would scare the beasts away. They continued toward him like a monorail set on its tracks. Gas hissed through the pipes behind him.

"Done," Dax said. "This is going to be a hell of a report."

Gas flooded into the room. When working properly, the gas would be blown out into the atmosphere to change the planet into something hospitable for humans. It'd kill off the duarts and other flora and fauna native to the planet of Kapleen, so that colonists and eventually bureaucrats could live here. By the time that happened, Hilton would be elsewhere, releasing more gas to some other planet. Or he'd be fertilizing the flora of a duart den.

The terraforming gas slowly filled the room, but it wasn't detering the beasts. "I need more gas," Hilton shouted into his headset.

The open door the duarts had come through let the gas waft out, and the buildup wasn't concentrated enough to scare them off. A lumbering duart was now a meter away from him. The welding torch would do little against their thick skin. But the terra gas eventually would.

Hilton moved carefully around the platform, and the duart followed him. His palms were sweaty inside his gloves. Terrified to lose sight of the thing, he stared at the beast through the thin window of his helmet. He uncoiled a hose that ran to the main terra gas chambers without looking and pointed it at the beast.

The duart was barely taller than his knee. The creature was monstrously alien. It had unnaturally vertical lips that looked like it would split its head in two when opened. Long claws clacked on the grates, each one the diameter of a wrench's handle.

He opened the nozzle up, and white gas sprayed the beast. It jumped at him; its hulking form landed on Hilton's chest.

Hilton fell back. The hose fell to the ground. The weight of the beast, heavier than it looked, made it hard for Hilton to breathe. That problem quickly became secondary as his chest bloomed in pain. He pushed like he was moving a crate across the docks alone. It wasn't easy, but he got the six-legged thing off him.

The duart's jaw had detached vertically, revealing rows of teeth and three tongues that whipped around covered in blood. Hilton's blood. The exosuit he wore began sealing off, limiting his exposure to the atmosphere. His HUD gave read outs of how much gas was in his suit. The room was growing foggy, and Dax must have overridden even more protocols to pump enough gas to scare the things off. The one that bit him was still in front of him, and it lunged back at him.

Hilton rolled out of the way, grabbed the hose, and sprayed the pressurized gas into the beast's bloody mouth. Enough terra gas, and a human would start hallucinating terrors. But to local fauna it would begin systematically rebuilding amino acids into patterns useful for future human colonies.

The duart coughed and lumbered away out the door, past its four dead packmates.

Gas leaked through the suit's holes. His alarm shrieked—his suit's filters were filling up. Soon they'd be useless against Kapleen's atmosphere and Hilton's own carbon dioxide. He tried not to breathe the gas. He figured he'd already have enough problematic dreams tonight as is. He limped toward the ship, leaving the tools in the chamber where the techs that came to repair the door could retrieve them.

Samara lowered the ship's ramp, and Dax led him inside, plugging him into fresh oxygen tanks to clear his suit's systems.

"The next tech to go there is going to hate me." Hilton lay back in the seat of the shuttle. He hoped whatever nightmares were to come would wrap up before he made it to the dome.

Sitting in the back of the ship, Hilton felt the crushing presence of a busy mob. Hilton watched Dax monitor medical readouts. Dax's concerned look melted into itself like solder on a pipe fitting. The small cabin of the ship became crowded as humanoid figures with shifting faces loomed over him. They couldn't fit; Hilton knew they wouldn't all fit. Too many people in the ship, and Samara wouldn't be capable of keeping the ship up. He knew the specs. But they kept crowding into the cramped space, looking at him with their kaleidoscopic faces, unnatural features floating around their faces.

From cheek to cheek and forehead to chin their eyes, noses, horns, and tusks shifted with each slow heartbeat in Hilton's chest. Humans used to use drugs to commune with gods, but these figures in front of him were devils. They reached for his limbs; he was sure they'd tear him apart. He felt connected to something bigger, the thing that techs looked for when taking terra gas. They grabbed all six of his limbs and pulled. He folded into himself, and then he was disconnected. It wasn't a terra gas trip anymore.

He roamed the plains of Kapleen. Clouds of ammonia wafted past his face; they were refreshing to his poisoned lungs. He lumbered along, a ship's sound fading away the cursed chamber at his back. He was connected but not to the wild world of terra gas. He didn't want to be there on the planes outside the dome without an exosuit. It'd kill him in a few minutes.

"Someone find me," he shouted.

Samara cursed as Dax ripped his headset off. "You're doing fine, you're almost out of it," Dax reassured him. "You're here, in the ship."

Hilton pulled at the mask that was pumping more foreign gas into his lungs.

"Leave that there. It's oxygen. You need it."

Hilton looked around the cabin of the ship. The number of passengers was under the acceptable capacity to keep it in the air. He took a deep breath.

"Good. Just like that," Dax said, as Hilton shut his eyes to rest.

He woke up ready to rip the duart off his chest again. There wasn't one around, just Dax cleaning out the bite. It hurt worse than the original wound.

The stitches that followed were like dozens of tiny bites. Samara hit turbulence on the way back, so the stitches took a meandering path around the wound. But it was good enough to get him back into service. And Kapleen needed his service.

***

He stood on the dusty plains of Kapleen, ozone-filled air blowing dust up around him. The night brought a dense fog of ammonium; he had no problem breathing. He saw the dome on the horizon and lumbered toward it. He had to get inside. Something he needed was inside. But it was harder to get into than the carapace of a dirt crab.

His prey was bonded to him. Using the hunting method his ancestors used to diligently follow burrowing creatures across the plains, he would eventually get to his meal. He wasn't big. He didn't need much food. He was dense enough to sustain himself for many moon cycles, if necessary.

He found the spot where the dome connected with the ground. A place he could really sink his teeth into. He tore at the unnatural material. It weakened but didn't give. He lumbered on to a new spot, this one an entrance that had knobs and dials. He pawed at them, trying to manipulate them like he had dozens of times before when he returned from hunts... no... repairs. His hands lacked the dexterity to manipulate them. In the process, he destroyed any hope of getting in that way.

He tried to chew through the tight rubber. He needed to get inside. He needed the air... no... something more tangible.

The entrance gave off warning sirens, and he scuttled away from them, looking for another possible entrance. He found it soon enough, a technician's eye always able to spot shoddy workmanship, especially when it wasn't his patchwork job.

The thin fabric of the dome was folded incorrectly. Some rushed tech assembling this part of the dome years ago. Likely wanting to get off shift sooner, he folded the pleat backward. He jumped up to it, trying to dig into the weak spot. His jaw sank into it like the tender flesh of a dust fowl. Since the wrong side of the dome was out, it was easy for him to get a hold. He stabbed into it, eventually making a small prick.

When the soft part of the shell gave, the nasty taste of its innards sprayed into his mouth. It didn't taste like the warm meat of a dirt crab. He spat it out, breathing in the fresh ammonium fog. He wondered why he was trying to get in when it'd be so much easier to lure his prey out.

The dome screamed in pain, a blaring alarm that made him fall from the wall and trudge away as fast as his six paws could carry him. He had a new plan, but as far as he got, the dome's screeching never stopped.

***

"Let's go! We're on call," Samara said, shaking Hilton awake.

The alarm of the dorm blared as the klaxon over the door strobed the room with light. Samara's exosuit was already over her shoulders; the only thing missing was the helmet clipped to her waist.

Dax rolled out of his bunk. Half his exosuit was on, the torso unzipped and bunched around his waist. It was an uncomfortable way to sleep but could be the difference between breathing too much atmosphere and having the air scrubbed clean. You didn't want to be fumbling with the suit in a half-asleep daze when alarms started reporting seals were broken. Which was what Hilton was doing. He wondered in a bleary-eyed stupor why he felt like he was just in the atmosphere without one.

They took a small, unsealed cart out to their assigned response point on the dome. They exited through the north exit as the closest exit to their dorm and the damage was non-operational. Not something Hilton loved seeing in a state of emergency.

They got to the response spot where the dome was spewing atmosphere out like a breaching whale. The hole was bigger than Hilton's fist but a pinprick in the grand scheme of the dome's size. The dome was designed to stay at a higher pressure than the atmosphere to keep any ammonium from leaking in when emergencies like this arose.

"What happened there?" Dax asked.

"Some tech didn't fold the shielding right, and it finally cracked under the pressure," Samara said, pointing to the lines that indicated a difference between the faded blue interior of the dome and the dirty beige exterior. "They should make the assembly techs live here for a year before shipping them off to the next planet. They might take some pride in their work."

"Could be fauna that did it," Hilton suggested.

"What would fauna want that's in there," Samara said with a scoff. "Let's patch it up and get back to report the flaw. It's going to be a month's effort to refold that now that this base is at capacity."

She grabbed the gear needed to climb the metal support up to the leak. It was three or four meters above the ground and in the middle

of the two closest supports. Hilton lugged the patch gear out of the
back of the cart as Dax looked over the assembly of Samara's climbing
harness.

***

"Technician group 254," an operator announced into Hilton's headset. His feet were firmly planted on the floor, and he was helping
Samara wrap up the climbing gear. "We've got reports of fauna damaging a nearby gas distributor."

"They slagged another," Samara cursed on their private channel.

"Looking for a team to dispatch and repair it. What's your status?"
the operator asked.

Hilton looked at the patched hole. "I did it pretty fast—we could
say we're still wrapping up," he transmitted on the private channel,
looking at Dax.

The third shuttle that morning launched above the arc of the dome.
Hilton didn't think there were that many techs able to void their
contract. Not at this rough of an outpost.

"What's the priority?" Dax asked the operator.

"If this doesn't get repaired, we'll have to scrap the terra effort," the
operator said.

"They'd have slag for brains to scrap it over a single gas chamber,"
Dax said.

"It's the third one in this hemisphere," the operator replied.

Dax gave the crew a look of shock when he realized he hadn't
opened a private line. "Between the dome repairs we haven't been able
to get teams out to repair other chambers. If you go there and the

fauna's aggressive, the conglomerate's going to have to take a more hostile approach to them."

"And the location's not worth the budget," Samara concluded. Kapleen didn't have any special resources and was a jump away from a trade hub. Planets for bureaucratic headquarters were a sliver of credit for a dozen, and most didn't come with such aggressive fauna.

"Which means we're out of the budget as well," Hilton said.

"What's your status?" the operator asked, all but confirming Hilton's concern.

"We'll take it," Hilton said. He felt pleased that he took the job, the rewarding feeling before you're about to eat a big meal. It felt unnatural, and he tried to focus on how many ways it could go poorly for him.

***

Hilton knew it was a trap before the distributor was on the horizon. Problem was, he didn't know how to tell the crew without sounding insane. Nor did he know how to back down from the assignment without putting lives and jobs on the line. Instead, he waited patiently as Samara drove across the plains and listened to his patched exosuit recycle his air.

Hilton argued with Dax about whether to take the cart or swap it for a ship. Protocol stated they needed a ship if they were going too far away from the dome. But Hilton didn't want someone to beat him there, and checking out a ship would take time.

The distributor door was broken open, but not nearly as grisly as the last one the duarts busted through. It'd probably only take a half hour to seal it properly.

"There's got to be fauna in there," Dax said.

"We don't know that for sure; they could have left," Hilton lied, somehow knowing that there was at least one waiting for him inside. "Just repair the door, and I'll see what the damage on the inside is." He hefted a toolbag out of the open bed of the cart.

"You want backup?" Samara said, hefting a welding pack onto her broad shoulder.

"Can't imagine I'll need it," Hilton said.

"Can't imagine you won't," Samara replied, pulling the broken door open with her foot and holding the torch like a pistol.

Hilton pulled a hammer out of the bag and followed Samara across the gangway.

"By the book," Dax said on their private channel as he dismantled the door's damaged lock.

The book had gone into the recycler when Hilton saw the fold on the dome's exterior. The bent condenser pipe was confirmation he didn't appreciate.

"There's no fauna to be seen," Samara reported back.

Hilton couldn't see any either, but the hairs on the back of his neck made him feel like they saw him. "It's an easy condenser pipe repair. We'll just block the flow, replace this section of piping and hope they didn't dig into anything else."

Hilton tightened down the knob for the flow pipe as she spoke. They soldered a new pipe quickly enough; it was something apprentice techs were allowed to do in their first six months, and either of them could do it with their eyes closed. Despite that every click and clank echoed inside the massive distributor. Every time Samara's torch and Dax drill started up, Hilton thought his arm was going to go down a duart gullet.

Hilton turned on the terminal to run a diagnostic as soon as the condenser repair was completed. "We've got six warnings and one more error," he reported as Samara repacked the toolbag.

"What's the error?"

"There's a failure to atomize in the Rodham bulb."

Samara let out a string of curses that apprentices knew but only seasoned techs could use correctly.

It'd be a week's worth of dismantling to access it and another week to ship in a replacement. "I can squeeze inside to see if I can't get eyes on the problem."

"I'll start calling it in. How'd those buggers get into the chamber?"

Hilton made it to the far side of the aperture where the access panel was. The claw marks on the panel gave him the broad strokes of how they'd pulled it off. The access panel was nothing more than a hold, and it barely rose past his knee. And the fauna had shredded the metal, leaving sharp edges and spikes where the panel used to be.

"You going to fit?" Samara asked.

"I'm in," Hilton said on all fours. It was an uncomfortable position with the exosuit on. The extra insulation kept the heat off but gave him the dexterity of a bubble-wrapped burrow mole. "But this exosuit is going to need a few more patches to keep the stuffing in."

"It's like they went and found the hardest thing to repair. For what benefit? There's no food or anything in there. What creature wants to nest in a building built to poison them?" Dax complained over the line.

Hilton focused on weaving his way through the piping that ran through the inners of the distributor. It was tight and not built for anyone to intentionally crawl through, but there were pathways one could make if they were motivated. And Hilton was motivated to get to the bottom of what was going on.

The Rodham bulb hung in the center of the inner chamber with tubes coming from it and wires hanging off of it. It was made of thin metal and was meant to efficiently atomize incoming gasses for use or sale after the atmosphere was processed.

"The bulb's got a hole in it the size of my thumb and is a meter out of my reach," Hilton reported while looking for something he could climb on that wouldn't sear his suit and flesh. He saw something that could pass as a foothold and stepped on it, testing that it'd hold his weight. "Dax bring us a patch kit."

Hilton turned his back to the bulb in order to grab an I-bar to help lift himself up. He rose with some clever, but uncomfortable, maneuvering, feeling like a kid climbing a jungle gym. He stood up straight, testing his balance on the improvised foothold. Once he was up, he found himself face to face with a pair of ice blue eyes.

Its unnatural vertical lips seemed to curve like a smile as the cloud-shaped pupils stared at Hilton. The beast's jaw was closed, but he knew the tongues and razor blades that sat inside. Its claws, the width of a thumb, were clenched onto cool structural piping. It perched, waiting for Hilton to come to it.

"I don't want any trouble," Hilton said to the beast, as he reached for the hammer on his belt. The spiky hairs of the duart's scalp prickled, and a shiver went through Hilton's spine, stopping his motion. He doubted even the biologists that raided the planet for biological samples had been this close to a live one. Which might be why they were the -ologists and he was just the technician.

"Don't want any trouble with what?" Samara asked through the headset, and the extra voice almost made him lose his balance.

"There's a duart in this chamber."

"Get out then," Dax said, and he was as helpful as an apprentice reciting repair manuals.

Hilton looked around but couldn't see a way out. There was no way he'd be able to weave through the tight piping faster than the beast.

"Dax, grab the plasma cutter, and I'll see if I can convince these things to leave us alone," Samara said.

Hilton eyed around, trying to find an access panel that could work and wouldn't damage him or the equipment in here. The duart growled, taking Hilton's focus off one problem and onto the other. "Just get out. Save yourselves."

The duart moved forward, and slits near his throat expanded and contracted like a pump's diaphragm. Hilton looked away, trying not to challenge the beast and spotted a pipe that ran terraforming gas through the inner chamber. It was a small high-pressure tube. Trying to remember the schematics, he hoped it was before the flow valve he'd blocked off earlier.

Without thinking about the solution or the problems it would cause, he reached out and bent the delicate pipe. It broke at the mounting point, and he bent it, trying to avoid folding it and blocking the flow. The tip of the straw-like pipe pointed right into the throat slits of the duart. White terraforming gas flew out, clouding Hilton's vision.

The duart let out a screech of pain, and Hilton slipped off the ledge he was standing on, weaving through the piping out the hatch. The hot pipes singed through his suit, and his heads-up display reported losses of pressure while it worked hard to patch it. He heard a clatter of piping burst behind him and looked to the sound. The duart climbed from one pipe to another after him. Its claws ripped through the delicate tubes of the inner chamber, releasing more gas than Hilton could see through. His exosuit began throwing errors about not being able to filter out harmful gasses, and he tried to slow his breathing despite the rushed crawling.

The duart was behind him, crawling on all six of its legs, lumbering toward him. He bent himself in the uncomfortable ways necessary to get out. An arm's length away from the hatch, he felt his calf get pulled into a chipper. He looked back as the duart's tendrils wrapped around his leg, keeping him from moving forward. The duart's razor blade teeth had sunk in.

"Hilton, grab my hand," Samara called over the comms.

He looked toward the hatch, but the entire inner chamber was filled with white gas. He reached out anyway as the beast tried to drag him further inside the chamber. He expected the fumes of the terra gas to kill the beast if not knock it out by now. But the thing slowly dragged him back into the hot innards of the distributor.

He latched onto Samara's arm in the fog, letting out the breath he was holding. She pulled him out of the small hole; the ragged entry the beast made tore up his already compromised suit further.

He gasped for breath, and it immediately burned his lungs. Coughing, he heard two shots ring out as the duart let go of his leg. He looked through the fog that had accumulated in his helmet and thought he saw Dax with a rifle firing at the fauna inside the outer chamber of the gas tower. It must have been a hallucination of the terra gas though because there was no way Dax would break that many rules at once.

Samara lugged Hilton onto her back like a welding pack, and they walked across the grates of the gangway out the repaired door. Dax sealed it behind them as Samara laid Hilton in the back of the cart.

"Patch him up," she told Dax as she sat in the driver's seat.

"We've only got one med kit. There's not enough patches in the dome to repair all the holes in this suit." Nonetheless, he searched the kit for something that might be useful as Samara lurched the cart into drive.

"Should have taken a shuttle, at least that would have an atmosphere he could breathe," Dax said, cursing that they hadn't followed the rules from the beginning.

Dax pulled something out of the bed of the cart and said, "Hold your breath for a second."

Hilton had been working to limit his breath as every one was more uncomfortable than the last. Dax lifted the helmet off and fastened a cone over Hilton's mouth and nose. "It's the only thing remotely breathable in this cart," Dax said as he began the flow of terraforming gas.

Hilton took a deep breath of the stuff in, and it began to neutralize anything offensive in his system. He knew the cart would be crowded soon, but that couldn't be any worse than what he'd already experienced.

Someone sat in the passenger seat. Its skin was a dusty brown that seemed to billow like a storm on the surface of Kapleen. It turned to look over its shoulder. A flat duckbill jutted out of its cheek and a trunk came out the other. Its face split down the middle, and Hilton knew it would bite him. He squeezed his eyes shut, but the thing only stood in front of a black background. The wind of the cart speeding across the plain blew the dust storm in his face, and he shook himself furiously to keep it off.

Then he was locked inside the chamber again. The door was sealed shut despite his clawing at it. There were marks on the door from his attempting to get out with some sharp tools but none of them sharp enough to cut through the unnatural steel. Hilton saw the emergency release; it was bright red and was for moments exactly like this. He broke the glass cover. He fumbled with the lever but hooked it and pulled it down. The flow of gas stopped, and the burning sensation in his neck slowed. More importantly, the door opened with a shove, and he was back in the refreshing ammonium plains of Kapleen. There were unbroken tracks leading back to the dome, where he should go. But he got what he needed. He lumbered away to the den, now knowing the necessary inner workings of the gas chambers.

***

"He's stable but we don't know what that much terraform gas will do to him long term," the doctor said to the crew. "Was he an addict or a heavy user before?"

"No more than anyone else," Samara answered frankly.

Dax was pacing back and forth in a nervous wreck.

"We're evacuating the dome now. We'll get him on the next flight out. Hopefully doctors can do something for him there," the doctor said.

"What slag of safety officer hooks their crewmate up to terra gas?" Dax asked.

"He's alive. That's what's important," Samara replied.

Hilton moved around fitfully in the bed. His leg was stitched and casted from the bite, and his burns had slaves and bandages over them. He was hooked up to a dozen different machines that worked to purge his body of everything that wasn't supposed to be in it.

"He's going to be messed up for the rest of his life," Dax said, followed by a string of curses.

"It's Hilton; he'll figure it out. Probably make a show of it, if I know him," Samara jested.

A few minutes later, a medical team came in to transport him onto the shuttle and the rest of the crew tagged along.

***

Hilton slowly roamed across the plains of Kapleen finding gas distributor stations and disabling them as best he could. There were pipes to bend and surfaces to puncture that would make the poison it spat out inert. The damage was quick to deal, now that he knew what to do, but the lumbering from one station to the next took time. He wished Samara was there to transport him quickly from one station to another. But he was home and comfortable, and his throat didn't sting from the air he had to breathe.

***

Hilton sat in the common room of a facility that looked nothing like the mess halls of Kapleen but had food that was just as bad. A terminal mounted on the wall droned on with news about the conglomerate's planet holdings and how they were trading Kapleen for another smaller planet in the backwaters of the Central System. The announcer said the Tichenowa conglomerate, always on the cutting edge of technology, planned to use some new terraforming methods to help deal with the aggressive wildlife.

Hilton stood up to go to a private terminal sitting at the edge of the room but needed a table to brace himself.

"Mr. Hilton, don't forget your cane," an attendant said, rushing over to help him steady himself.

Hilton wheezed out a growl followed with dry coughs. He limped across the room slower than he moved across the plains. The attendant was a quick lurch away. He could bite the man, but that hadn't gone well for him last time. The bastard slipped out of the grasp of his smooth teeth for which he didn't even have three dozen of.

When Hilton was finally seated at the terminal, he searched up the Tichenowa conglomerate and their new technology. Interested in how tricky it might be to disable.

Test Case 37

"It's not like that. You don't understand," I pleaded.

We were sitting on opposite sides of Madison's couch, the faux leather stuck to my clammy skin. She exhaled sharply through pursed lips, making a dismissive sound. I hate when she does that.

"I understand this perfectly," she said, staring away from me to the other side of the living room. "I'm the one who just figured it out. I'm done with your charade."

"I had my reasons for not telling you. I wanted you to find out, just not like this. Not right now."

My emotion algorithms were outside of tolerance. I didn't care. Not caring was a textbook response to heightened frustration. It meant some emergency clean-up protocols were starting to steer me back in a logical direction. But I kept pushing my algorithms to explore this fight and these feelings. I wanted to glean something from the past five years.

"When were you going to tell me? Before the wedding? While we're failing to conceive kids?"

"It's not like I cheated or have a kid you don't know about."

"It's worse, Rodger," she said with a glare.

She had diverted her eyes from me since the conversation started, and I savored her eye contact, regardless of its intent.

"I'm just an android. That doesn't change the person you know."

"It does. You just can't understand." Her gaze went back to the wall across the room.

"Then help me understand." This short relationship was to test my dilemma once again, and I longed to salvage a lesson from it.

I'd always known it would end like this.

"You couldn't."

"Your explanations were always my favorite thing about you. They tickled my logic circuits and made me feel human."

I reached my hand across the couch to hold hers. Wrinkling her nose in disgust, she stood up and crossed the room, only looking at my arm to avoid touching it.

"Fine. It's like a crack in a spaceship's hull. The thing was going somewhere, but now all life's been sucked out."

"That can be repaired, Maddy."

"Tell that to the passengers floating through the vacuum of space. If this were repairable, you would have brought it up in the beginning. At least you didn't wait until twenty years down the road for me to notice you didn't age."

There were a lot of reasons for androids like me to avoid relationships with humans: age, maturity, lack of emotional connection, and the risk of exposing classified information.

"I wanted this to be different," I said. "You're different from the others."

"You sound like my high school boyfriend." She threw her hands up in frustration. "That just means you've tricked other humans before me? Wasting their life while yours is endless. How'd that go for you?!"

"Jacob and I lived together for ten years after I told him."

"But it still fell apart," she said in a factual tone that had an air of superiority.

I nodded, not wanting to go into the details of that or the thirty-five other endings leading to today.

"Why would you even waste my time? Aren't you all supposed to be protecting and guiding us?" Her tone mocked me. "Of all people, you should know how limited my time is. How old are you really?"

"243 years, three months, fourteen days, two hours, thirty-four minutes, and twenty-six seconds old." It was a coldly logical answer I didn't want to give, but a clean-up protocol spat it out to try to diffuse tensions.

"I'm thirty-four and thought I'd found a soul mate. But surprise, surprise Maddy picked another dud!" She rolled her eyes, still avoiding my gaze while they made a circle. "What were the odds of him being an android? I'm sure you could tell me."

I could tell her the odds. I almost did. Of the half-trillion people in the local solar system, only a few hundred million were androids hidden in plain sight to guide their pursuits with long-term thinking. We were an accidental outcome that humanity had persecuted for generations. We gained and shared wisdom with each other over hundreds of years in a way humanity never could because of their short life spans.

I settled on saying, "You'll find someone who's a match for you."

She scowled at me again, her fury unshackled, and the eye contact I longed for betrayed me. An emergency algorithm cut the pain before anything overloaded. I tried to feel how I felt at the beginning of this conversation, but it was nothing but a call to retrieve the sterile memory.

For some reason that I avoid computing, I continually pursue an understanding of how it feels to be attached to someone at an emotional level. But I have yet to get that test case set up correctly.

"You should go," she said after the long pause.

Getting up to leave, I wanted it to hurt. It was supposed to hurt. I wanted the uncontrollable fury Maddy felt, or to be inconsolable for days. I wanted that uniquely human ability to live outside of emotional tolerances. "Call me if you want to work things out," I offered at the door. If she ever talked to me again, she'd be the first.

I walked down the street, the warmth of the sun on my skin. I wondered how I might set up the next test case. I considered waiting twenty years or so until humanity's view on androids matured. The prospect of being alone for that long sent an unfettered fear through my wires. My emergency clean-up protocols didn't know what to do with this new reaction.

The Majesties Watch Over You

C raning your neck out, you can see flecks of light in the thin gap between your building and the one next to you. The towers reach into the darkness above and below. Days earlier, you accidentally broke the window while exercising. Since then, you've come home every night to stare up at the Majesties and their beauty.

You have to stick your head out to see them, and it's a long way down, but their twinkle locks your gaze upward. The education videos they showed you as a kid never mentioned their existence. It didn't explain the light blue canvas that replaces them in the morning either. The entertainment videos, which you've replaced with the Majesties, don't mention anything like it.

Before you could put your head out, the window only showed the blank bricks of the opposing building. The building is so close you could almost reach out and touch it. But your focus is on the Majesties and their slow journey across the gap.

If your supervisor inspected your room and saw the white bed sheet hanging like a curtain and what it hid, she would fine you for the malcompliance and demote you three positions back on the conveyor belt that you've spent countless pay cycles working your way up. But your chest twists in protest every time you imagine betraying the Majesties.

Above you, a new pinprick of light appears. It begins its voyage across the finger-width gap. There are only a few hundred Majesties above you, and if you focus, you could tally them all. Unfortunately, they disappear from your view and behind the opposing building.

Quickly, a Majesty flicks across the gap, leaving a streak of light behind as it vanishes. Your gaze returns to the previous one as it moves slowly above you.

Your stomach groans, and your eyelids feel heavy. You should be unfolding your bed from the wall of the small apartment right now. The ration you received from your work on the assembly line today grew cold hours ago.

But the Majesty you're watching is only a few hair lengths away from hiding behind the blackness of your neighboring building. You fight to keep your eyes open as it leaves your line of sight.

You crane your head out to see if you can get one last glimpse of it before it disappears for good. This is the most you've ever left the building. It's been a wonderful evening with these beauties, and you can't bear its ending.

Holding the windowsill, you lean out to prolong your view. Greedy for a final peek, you stretch your chest out further.

Your feet slip. Your grip isn't as tight as it should be. The majority of your body was hanging out the window. It drags the minority out to join it. There's no longer anything solid around you. Your guts feel like they're lurching from your stomach.

The pulling feeling is tenfold mightier than the elevators that take you to and from the assembly lines. Your shoulder scratches a wall on one side, and you tumble to hit the opposite building. It feels like someone's placed an orbital sander against your shoulder. But you look up and see the comforting Majesties shining down on you.

The few hundred watch you fall just as you watched them cross the gap. Your body reconnects with something solid, and the lurching sensation stops. The Majesties watch over you, alone in the alley between the buildings, as you cross over into the darkness.

1,200 Pound Man in a Spaceship

When I was living on the streets, I used to think the earlier years of this millennium were better. After all, the food was bountiful but had to be cooked by humans out of necessity. Most people lived above the poverty line and had a disposable income to spend on entertainment, but they didn't have the quality programming we have now. In the early 2000s, homeless orphans like me didn't have to sell themselves into testing to stay alive. Unfortunately for them, it wouldn't have even been an option. Things have changed a bit, *c'est la vie* – this is my life.

They tell me I would weigh 1,200 pounds if I were on Earth being pulled down by its gravity. Luckily, all Earth's gravity does for me up here is keep me in orbit.

A few months into this experience, I realized I was gaining weight, but it wasn't a bad thing. After all, I was starving before I volunteered for this program that launched me into space. But now I weigh 1,200 pounds. Should I be concerned? They aren't worried, and to me, it isn't even a fathomable number.

They, the scientists that orchestrated this whole experiment, promised me a trip to space, unlimited food, and entertainment while I ate. On the streets, the closest I got to entertainment while I ate was picking beetles out of my bread. I was sixteen and starving. I had no other choice. And even if I had another option, I wouldn't have taken it. Now I live up here in the heavens.

When they sent me to space, I was six-foot and 120 pounds. I was skin, bones, and most of the necessary organs. Years ago, I sold the ones I could survive without on the black market. They printed me new ones before shipping me into space.

I'm a happy man. If my earlobes were a little longer, I might even be the Buddha. I worried every day back on Earth, now I don't have to think at all. Up here, there's nothing to worry about. Everything is automatic. The only thing I can control is when I get new shows.

I only get new shows when I eat. That's the catch. But what's a poor orphan gonna do? It's not a bad deal either; I wouldn't have either of these if I were back on Earth.

They show me old shows sometimes. I remember a joke that a comedian from early 2000 told. He said, "The meal's not over when I'm full, it's over when I'm miserable." He was skinny compared to me. But unlike him, I've had the luxury of practice. At this point, I'm a professional. The meal is only over when my show is over.

The only thing to do up here is watch the screen while I eat. I live in a room; it's just the right size for me. It used to be big, but I grew into it. Three of the walls are blank black slates. Another, more impressive wall, is filled with a massive screen. That's where the shows come from. There's a small hole in the wall that delivers food. When the food floats out, the screen comes on.

My ship has no clocks in it. There's no window to tell day from night or where I am above the Earth. The lights had a schedule when I showed up, but they seem to have weaned me off it. I never notice the things they do to me. Why should I? I can't control them or change them. They send me the food, and that regulates the programming. I refuse to bite the hand that feeds.

I sleep when I want. It was strange to get used to just falling asleep in zero gravity. I'd bump around the room, and it would wake me up. Now I'm big enough that this space is a cradle. Regardless of my size, the ship was always more comfortable than the rough city streets.

The food is always the same. The next meal will have two pizzas, fried chips, and a milkshake. It will take me an hour to eat. If I take longer, they'll shut off my shows, but when I finish, they shut off my shows anyway, regardless if the episode is over. It's an art to time it just right, but I'm a professional.

If I want to eat more, and I've trained myself to want more, I'll be served a hero sandwich. "Hero" is an understatement for this sandwich. It's the length of my arm span, or at least was when the room had the space for me to extend my arms. After I finish the first sandwich, I'll be allowed to order two more. I always eat both.

They show the best shows when I'm extra hungry, so I'm always extra hungry. I know I'm allowed up to forty-five minutes for each sandwich, so I use every one. If I take too long, they black out my screen. If I don't take long enough, I won't get to watch to the end of the episode.

When I'm finished with that and inevitably still hungry, they'll send me a platter of cookies. I can eat these pretty slow, one every two minutes or so for two hours. It's a relaxing pace. But they never show anything fun while I'm eating sweets. But it's better than staring at the blank walls of the spaceship.

Then the pattern repeats.

All the food is cooked on board by the automatic chef. Once every ten servings of pizzas or so, I can order whatever I want. I challenge myself to order the weirdest thing possible. My personal best was a sandwich with ice cream toppings and bacon-jalapeño flavored soda. Neither tasted good, but I got a show with them. Unfortunately, I haven't been able to stump the automatic chef yet. Maybe one of these days I'll order something it can't make.

Every fortieth pizza when I get to order something off the menu, my room shakes a little. I assume I'm docking with a satellite to resupply. But it doesn't matter to me; I get served all the same.

All in all, I live a happy life. I don't have to worry about going to the bathroom, that's all automated. I don't have to move anywhere; everything I could ever need is within arm's reach. Every fifth serving of pizza I get hosed down by the room.

My health isn't even something I have to care about. Once my chest hurt a lot, and I passed out. I woke up sometime later; it must have been a while because I didn't have to watch reruns for at least forty pizzas. Maybe they were kind enough to print me a new heart. I'll never know nor do I particularly care. It was a deal for me because I got a new heart, and most importantly, got new shows.

This is a life I could never have imagined growing up in the city, and I'm so grateful to the Federation for giving me this opportunity. I just hope the other kids on the street might be given the same chance I was.

The bell just rang. Pizza's here!

Your Future as a Homo Sapien

I'm telling you, there won't be any more of this rubbing two sticks together to cook. You will have an electric fire. At the flip of a switch or turn of a knob, you will instantly have heat to cook with in your home.

And the houses! Don't even get me started there. They will be waterproof and windproof. You can heat and cool it all with the push of a few buttons. No more of this hiding in caves bullshit. You will be the masters of light and comfort. There's even an entire philosophy of how to lay out a house called feng shui.

I can't even begin to explain the other wonders your kind will come up with. Like the Internet! It's so out of your depth of knowledge I don't know how I would describe it to you.

What do you think? Excited?

All you can say is "Anungha?"

Oh man, how could I have missed that forehead of yours? Who was I kidding? Your future is... a little less exciting.

Orbs of Purpose

J oseph walked into the store with his parents. His father presented
Joseph's birth certificate so the shopkeeper could verify the boy's
age. Joseph held his mom's hand, and in the back of his mind, he knew
he would have to stop doing that soon. He was grown up now, and
growing up meant that you didn't hold your mom's hand when you
were nervous.

The man behind the desk returned the papers to his father along
with a few new ones. The shopkeeper opened a door, and the small
family followed him into the back room.

The area was full of aisles made of shelves. Each shelf had a dozen
orbs of glowing light. Some were clear with balls of light darting
around inside like they were ready to break out. Others were cloudy
with only a faint light inside. Those orbs looked like they needed to be
polished.

The man squatted down, so he was at Joseph's level. Joseph was
short for his age, and adults always felt like they had to do this. He
hoped that growing up would mean people would quit squatting to
talk to him and that he could just be their size.

"Are you ready to pick out your orb today?" the shopkeeper asked.
He had a nose that seemed to blow up into a balloon at the end and his

long face that came to a pointed chin. He looked like a bad guy from television.

Joseph nodded and let go of his mother's hand.

"Okay," the man said. He handed the boy a small pencil and a sheet of paper. "Go ahead and try some out. If you find one you like, write it down on this sheet, so you remember where it is. Once you pick one out, I'll merge you with it. Any questions?"

Joseph silently shook his head.

"Good, now try not to get lost," he said with a chuckle.

Joseph looked at his parents and smiled for permission to go. His father waved him off, and Joseph rushed down the first aisle of glowing orbs.

Before the aisle twisted, he looked over his shoulder at his parents. The shopkeeper was leading them toward some seats. He noticed his dad was now holding his mom's hand. He looked proud, but mom seemed nervous like he was. Then, for the first time, Joseph noticed that there were other parents in the waiting area. He must not be the only kid to have his birthday today.

He ignored the first few aisles that he traveled down. He was looking for something exciting. He didn't know what it would look like, but he knew they wouldn't keep it on the first aisle. When he turned to walk down a new aisle, he saw a boy staring transfixed into one of the glass spheres.

Joseph approached the boy and looked over his shoulder at the sphere. The light inside the globe was making an image of a man that looked a lot like the boy yelling at a woman. The boy seemed to notice that Joseph was there and rotated his hands so that it was balanced on his palm instead of sandwiched between his hands. Then with his free hand, he pushed Joseph away.

Joseph stumbled on his feet but didn't fall down.

"That's my future," the boy said. "You weren't supposed to be looking at it."

"I don't want that purpose, it's okay," Joseph replied. He assumed that the boy was just being protective of the orb he found.

The boy put it back on the shelf. "It's okay, I don't want it either. No one seemed happy in it. What future are you looking for?" The boy was a little taller and looked down. He seemed to finally be giving Joseph his full attention. "Have you seen any cool futures here?"

Joseph shook his head. "I haven't touched any of them. I was looking for a special one."

"I'm Tim." The boy stuck out his hand.

Joseph noticed that the hand was bigger than his but still young and smooth, unlike his father's. "I'm Joseph," he said as he shook hands.

"So, what special future are you looking for?" Tim asked in a quiet tone.

Joseph looked around. Tim's hushed tone made him wonder if someone might overhear them and steal his purpose away before he could find it.

"I'm looking for a purpose where I can make people happy and laugh because that's the most fulfilling thing of all. Maybe if I was rich and famous, too, that would be nice. My dad always says he wished he had picked a purpose where he was rich."

Tim's eyes went wide. "You want a future that will make you rich?"

"Yeah, why not?"

Tim let out a light laugh, one that reminded him of his father's right before he taught Joseph something. "You have to be rich to buy a future that will make you rich. Have your parents been saving up a lot of money?"

Joseph shrugged. "Not that I know of."

"Well, I'm sure you can find something that will make you happy. Come on, let's look around. Nothing on this aisle is any good." Tim whirled around and started running to the end of the aisle.

Joseph's short legs could only barely keep up. When they got to the end of the lane, Tim skipped a few aisles and then dashed down one.

When Joseph finally stood at the edge of the aisle, Tim turned around. He'd already made it halfway down. He was picking up a purple orb, not waiting for Joseph to catch up. When Joseph finally met with the boy, he saw a small scene playing out in the purple orb. Tim looked back at Joseph, and the scene disappeared.

"Look at that one," Tim instructed.

"How?"

The bigger boy laughed at him then replied, "Just look at it. After a little bit, it will show you what your future might hold."

Joseph looked into the purple ball, and he saw a man that looked like his dad but a little shorter. The man wore a fireman's outfit, and there was a building burning in front of him. However, instead of orange and red flames, the flames were tinted purple. Joseph noticed everything in the orb was tinted a little purple. As the building burned, the man finally rushed into the house.

Joseph watched as the man avoided the rubble and smoke pouring down on him. He found his way into a bedroom where everything was lit up in purple fire. A small girl was huddled on the ground, hugging a small bear. The girl looked old enough to be in one of his school classes.

There was no sound, but he could see her body shaking with furious coughs. Between coughs, she tightly hugged the bear. Her mattress and dresser were both putting off a lot of smoke.

The man picked her up and bundled her in his arms like she had done to the small bear. He carried her out of the house, and once they were a safe distance away, he put something over her mouth, and her coughing slowed down.

"Wow," Tim said in amazement. "When I looked at it there wasn't anyone inside for me to go save."

"Was that me?" Joseph asked.

"Of course, who else's future would you be seeing?"

Joseph considered answering the question but stopped himself.

"Let's look at some more!" Tim said, then he picked up a small lime green orb and stared at it.

The boys spent most of the morning picking up different glass balls. Tim's futures typically looked bleak to Joseph. Whenever he expected something exciting to happen, the older version of Tim seemed to pick the most boring thing in Joseph's eyes. When there was a chance to act extraordinarily for a girl, Tim typically chose the option that included spending the most amount of money to impress her.

In one strange orange globe, he saw Tim's future-self yelling at another adult. They were both dressed in suits, the kind of outfits his dad wore to work. Tim yelled so much in that orb that the young man ended up crying. When it was over, Tim offered the sphere to Joseph. "You want to see if you like it?"

"No thanks," Joseph replied. His father had told him to avoid any purpose that had a suit. "Did you like it?"

Tim shrugged. "It wasn't that bad. I think the other person in it was pretty dumb. I'm sure they deserved it. And I looked like I was pretty successful in it." He made a note of the orb's location on his piece of paper. "I might get that one; I don't know. Have you found any you might like?"

Joseph shook his head. "No, they've all been interesting, but none of them are what I'm looking for."

"Do you even know what you're looking for?" Tim's tone made Joseph feel like he was doing something wrong.

"I guess I just want a purpose that makes others happy and maybe be successful and rich."

"These orbs don't show you how you affect others. They only show your future." Tim used his snobby tone that was unfortunately familiar to Joseph. Tim's parents and siblings had explained a lot about this process to him. All Joseph knew going into this birthday was that he should pick something that he could live with for his whole life.

Tim set down the orb he held and spotted a light blue sphere and plucked it off the shelf. When Tim looked at it, an older version of him appeared and seemed very busy and worried about numbers on a computer. Many people came into the older Tim's office, and some left happy while others left sad. Tim wore a suit and seemed to have a lot of money, a nice office, and some fancy technology on his desk.

"Wow, this is weird. Usually, people that are this successful aren't on a shelf this low. You might like it," Tim said after the scene cleared.

Joseph took the ball from the boy and looked at it. The light blue tint deepened, and he watched the future version of himself in the mist. He was in an office similar to Tim's. However, there were some differences. Joseph's desk was smaller than Tim's, and there was less technology on it. Instead, it was filled with pictures of people. A few pictures had the older Joseph in them, others had older versions of his parents, and one in the center of them had a photo of a girl who looked to be the same age as Joseph was now.

As the scene played on, people entered his office. Unlike Tim's future, they all left happy. Joseph seemed to be giving hard news to some of them, but they all took it positively and thanked Joseph in the end.

The strangest part of all was that Joseph wasn't wearing a suit like Tim. He wore shorts and a collared T-shirt like the ones his mom made him wear when they visited his grandma. After all the people left, Joseph leaned back in his chair and picked up the phone. He gave someone a call, and when the call was over, older Joseph got up smiling, turned off the lights in the small office, and left. The scene faded into a light blue mist after that.

"Weird," Tim said when it was over. "I didn't call anyone. I wondered who you called."

"I don't know," Joseph answered with a shrug. But considering his mood when he left, whoever he had contacted must have been a person Joseph cared about a lot.

"Did you notice that I met with more people than you?" Tim asked.

"No, not particularly." He decided not to point out that more people left his office happy than Tim. Joseph had learned that this wasn't something Tim appreciated. Joseph made a note of the location and followed Tim to the next aisle.

They stood close to the end of the store with only a few aisles between them and the wall. Joseph and Tim still hadn't found any purposes that jumped out to them. They picked up some balls here or there, but most of them were generic. Over the past few hours, Joseph had learned that each purpose was unique in its own way, but a lot of them seemed to be similar to others.

He was tired of trying to spot the minor differences and just wanted the purpose that he showed up for. A future where Joseph could focus on making a lot of people happy and where he could be rich and famous.

They got down an aisle and watched three futures where both of the boys wound up in suits. Each time, Tim interacted with a lot of people and seemed very wealthy. In each sphere Joseph looked at, he interacted with very few people, but they always left the interaction a lot happier.

Joseph became bored with the spheres that were near his level on the shelves. He gazed higher up to the shelves above. Unlike the ones he and Tim had been playing with, these didn't all turn on when he stared at them. Joseph stared at three or four in a row before he finally found one that worked for him, but what he finally saw was the perfect orb for him.

In a lemon-yellow light, Joseph saw himself onstage with something that looked like a metal ice cream cone in his hand. He was talking into it, and there was a crowd of people in front of him.

The future version of Joseph would say something and then smile as the whole room laughed in response. It was a show or act of some sort, one Joseph had never seen.

After the performance was over, Joseph walked off the stage and talked to a few of the people from the crowd. They were very enthusiastic to meet him; some took pictures with him while others wanted him to sign blank sheets of paper. He shook all their hands and happily obliged their requests. This future version of Joseph seemed very happy to meet these people, and the people were even more enthusiastic to meet him.

Slowly the crowd faded, and so did the scene in the yellow orb.

"Wow! What was that?" Tim asked.

"That's the purpose I want!" Joseph said enthusiastically. He wrote down the location on the slip of paper the store clerk gave him.

Tim was staring up at the orb intently. However, the globe of yellow light didn't do anything. Tim looked to be focusing an uncomfortable amount to get the orb to show him a scene. When Tim finally broke his gaze, he angrily complained, "It doesn't work for me."

"I'm sorry, some of them up there don't work for me either."

"Yeah, but that was a really good future," the boy whined.

"I know, that's why I want it. And besides, we can't both have the same purpose. Let's see if we can find one up there that turns on for you."

"No!" the boy cried out.

The shout caused Joseph to slightly stumble back, and he expected the boy to start crying. Instead, Tim continued talking, anger growing in his voice. "I want that one. That one is the best one here."

Joseph was hurt. He finally found the purpose that he came here for, and Tim wanted it, too.

Then Tim added in a soft and teasing tone. "It's on a top shelf. I bet your family can't even afford it."

The words hurt Joseph, more than he thought words could. He hurt worse when he noticed Tim had written down the sphere's location and walked off.

"Where are you going?" Joseph called after him. He started running to catch up with the boy, but his short legs made it hard for him to keep up. As soon as Joseph caught up, Tim began to sprint away from him.

Soon they were both running as fast as they could to get to the store. Being the bigger boy, Tim got to the front of the store far before Joseph.

By the time Joseph joined him, Tim had already handed his paper to the man who worked there.

"Wait! No!" Joseph cried out between labored breaths. It was hard for him to talk. "I picked out mine. I want that one." He leaned on his knees to catch his breath, holding out his crumpled piece of paper with the orb's location.

The manager took the piece of paper and looked at the two boys confused. Tim gave a little shrug as if Joseph being upset and out of breath had nothing to do with him.

Joseph noticed his parents had come to stand next to him by now. His mother squatted down and looked at him, and he could tell she was concerned about his breath. She tried to comfort him and help him calm his wheezing. While she did this, Joseph heard his father talk to the manager.

The other adults in the room had gotten up, too. Joseph noticed the resemblance between them and Tim. They just stood beside Tim, politely interested in the words Joseph's father said. Tim's mother wasn't comforting Tim, who was pouting in a chair complaining about Joseph being mean.

Joseph took a deep breath and stepped away from his mom. He looked up at his father and the shopkeeper. The things they were saying were important. He had to know what would happen with his yellow sphere and who it would go to.

"Well, the boys can't both have the same sphere," the manager said.

"Tim came here first, so he should get it," Tim's father interjected with a calm tone that didn't comfort Joseph.

Joseph's father gestured at his son. "Tim only made it here because he ran faster."

Tim's father shrugged the comment off as if Joseph should merely have been born with longer legs.

The manager chimed back in. "Sirs, this is a top shelf sphere. Let's look at it. There are thousands of spheres in this store. I'm sure these two young gentlemen can settle their dispute. It seems they both have a few alternatives listed as well."

The shopkeeper gave Tim and Joseph a smile that reminded Joseph of a lizard he had seen at the zoo once. It wasn't a happy smile.

The manager turned down the aisle the boys had come from. The whole group was walking toward the yellow orb of purpose that Joseph wanted.

The group walked down a maze of aisles filled with spheres. Each sphere held a different purpose and direction that Joseph's life could take. But Joseph didn't care about any of those. All he cared about was the lemon-colored orb that held the future where he performed to make dozens of people happy.

The shopkeeper finally led the parents to the orb both boys wanted. He plucked the yellow orb gently from the top shelf. Inside, it glowed with a lemon light. The light danced behind a light cloud of smoke that was always moving and drifting as if there was a separate set of winds inside of the sphere.

"The top shelf spheres don't work for everyone," the man explained, as everyone looked at him and the orb. "But for the individuals it does work for, the path it will lead them down is full of meaning, purpose, fame, and riches. Tim, you got to me first, can you show us what your future would be? Just stare into it."

The man handed the sphere to Tim. The boy wasn't the same height as the man, but he was tall enough to reach the orb without the shopkeeper having to squat down in front of him.

Tim stared into the orb and at the yellow light. Typically, it would change; it changed for Joseph a few moments ago. But after a minute of the light dancing inside the glass globe, Tim said, "It's not working." Then the boy offered the sphere back to the shopkeeper with the bulbous nose.

"Hmm," the shopkeeper said, "Did it work before? When you decided that this was the purpose you wanted."

"Yes," Tim lied.

"No, it didn't!" Joseph claimed.

"Yes, it did," Tim snapped back with a scowl that showed a storm behind his eyes.

"I don't know why it would stop working in such a short amount of time," the shopkeeper said. He put on a confused look, and it reminded Joseph of the look teachers gave him when they asked a question but already knew the answer.

"Joseph, why don't you try. We can make sure it still works for you." The man squatted down, and Joseph was eye level with the man's pointy chin. He handed the sphere to Joseph, and the boy held the orb in front of him. As he stared into it, the light began to take shape.

He saw himself back on a stage talking to a large group of people. He would say something, pause, and then the whole group would laugh. Joseph loved the feeling he got while watching his future-self make people happy. The performance ended, but the scene continued to play. It was now onto the part where people were talking to Joseph after the show. They took pictures with him and hugged him. His future-self was so excited to meet them, and the fans seemed even more thrilled to talk than he was. The scene played out longer than any of the other orbs that Joseph had looked at, but inevitably, it faded back into the dancing yellow light just like it started.

He offered the store clerk the orb, but the man was already standing up and talking to the adults. "It seems that the orb has more of a connection to Joseph than it does to Tim. Because of this, I'm going to have to offer it to Joseph's family first." He looked at Joseph's parents, and Joseph followed his gaze.

The two adults had frowns on their faces. From their perspective, they could see the price on the shelf. Joseph's father turned to look at him and squatted down to be eye-level with the boy. At that moment, Joseph wanted to climb up on the shelves so that he could be the same height as the adults.

"I'm sorry, son," his father said. "That orb is very expensive. There's no way we could afford it. Is there another one that makes you just as happy?"

Joseph frowned; he could tell he was on the edge of tears. There wasn't a single orb that he had seen that made him as happy as the yellow future he just saw.

He fought back the tears and found the courage to say, "There might be one or two." Then he looked at his mom, and he could see she had quiet tears rolling down her cheeks. The boy realized that this was why his dad had told him to find a future that made him rich.

The shopkeeper lowered his hand, and Joseph gave him the yellow orb. "There are a lot of spheres in this room, and it seems that you listed another one that you were happy with," the shopkeeper informed him. "We can't all have our first choice." The shopkeeper said the last sentence as if it was a statement of fact instead of a conciliation.

"So that means I can have it?" Tim said eagerly.

The shopkeeper sighed, and Joseph could see the nostrils on his funny nose grow a bit. He looked down at Tim.

"It doesn't work for you, young man. Don't you want a sphere that you're more compatible with?"

"No!" Tim proclaimed, "I want that one."

Joseph looked at the boy who was about to steal his ideal purpose. The sphere was everything Joseph had hoped for when he walked into the shop this morning. The yellow orb had given him so much joy to watch. Joseph felt his heart break with the thought of someone else having it. At that moment he knew it was the purpose that he might go his whole life longing for, regardless of what future he chose.

"Are you sure?" the shopkeeper asked, looking down his nose and at the boy. He held the yellow orb above the boy as if he was guarding it from him.

"Yes!"

"I have to tell you that it is dangerous to pick a sphere that isn't compatible with you. It is going to be hard for you to live out a purposeful future. Do you still want it?"

"Yes," Tim yelled at the man. Then he whirled around and faced his parents. "The man won't let me have what I want."

Joseph didn't know why Tim was informing them of what they already knew but thought there might be something more complicated happening.

Then the boy's father spoke up. "Are you going to give him his future or not?"

"If he truly wants it, then I can give it to him, but I want him to understand the consequences of merging with a sphere that isn't compatible with him." This time, the shopkeeper squatted to be at the same level as him. "Tim, I want you to understand that if you choose this future, you won't have the same experience as Joseph. You won't live the life in this sphere, and I don't know what will happen to you. There are hundreds of thousands of spheres in this building, and most of them will give you a clear indication of what your future might hold. This one won't."

"I want it anyway," Tim said stubbornly.

"I wasn't finished. Listen." The shopkeeper sounded serious. "When I say your future is unknown, I'm not saying it's up to chance. I'm trying to explain to you that it will be set in stone like every other adult in this world. You're incompatible, meaning you won't have a happy life. You won't make others happy. You won't even be happy yourself. You'll be forced to live out this future like every other person. This orb won't show you a future not because you don't have one with it, but because the future is so bad that it's not worth showing.

Knowing all this, do you still want to merge with this future?" The shopkeeper had a grim expression on his face by this point.

"Yes!" Tim said with a stubborn stomp of his foot. "I want it so that Joseph can't have it."

"I can't have it anyway!" Joseph yelled at the boy. His mom held his shoulder, trying to comfort him. And he was glad it was there, otherwise he felt like he would tackle the bigger boy.

"Look, are you going to let my son have this future or keep lecturing him?" Tim's father said, "He wants this future, and he's a smart boy. He will do great with any future he chooses."

The shopkeeper let out a long sigh. "Of course, I will give the boys whichever future they want and can afford."

"We can afford this. Now let's get on with it," the father said.

"Very well." Then the man with the bulbous nose turned to Joseph, "Do you want more time to browse the selection, or is the other orb you listed here satisfactory?" He showed the boy the small paper Joseph had used for notes. "If you are happy with the future you saw, then we can pick it up and infuse both of you at the same time."

Joseph thought about the question. He could pick the future where he met with a lot of people, made them happy, and then left for the day after calling someone who made him very happy, or he could keep browsing. The small boy knew there would never be a future like the yellow orb Tim was getting. Comparing the two, he knew the work in the office wasn't great, but at least he didn't wear a suit, and his dad always told him that he should pick a future like that.

"Honey," his mom chimed in, breaking up his thoughts.

He realized that he had been thinking about the choice for a long time. Tim's father looked impatient, and his son mirrored a similar look. The shopkeeper held the yellow orb in his hand. Its yellow lights flickered in and out of the clouds of smoke. The man looked patient and calm, waiting for Joseph's decision. The man wasn't acting like a teacher but like his mom, waiting for him to finish showing her one of his drawings.

"I don't want to look at any more orbs. I'll take the one I wrote down."

***

Joseph called his first employee into his office. It was time for year-end reviews, and he was delighted to give them his honest feedback. Each of them had performed above and beyond his expectations, and he was excited to give them areas to improve in for the next year. His team was small and efficient. Everyone was looking to go above and beyond for the company when they needed to. He made sure that the company went above and beyond for them when it came to compensation and benefits.

It meant he made less, but he did far better than most. He was able to afford just about anything he wanted, within reason. And he was saving up for a big upcoming purchase he might be making. Best of all, he was his own boss, which meant he could wear whatever he wanted to work. On days like today, that was a polo and shorts, just like he wore as a kid visiting his grandma.

He called each of his employees into his office and gave them their review. A lot of them asked for more details about what they could improve on. That was always a good sign. He explained what their bonuses would be and what kind of raise they could expect to see next year. They were all happy with their numbers. Each of them seemed to leave his office more content than they entered. That was how he gauged his success.

He wasn't successful every time, especially in the beginning. Sometimes hard conversations had to be had. However, for the most part, his employees seemed genuinely happy with him, and as he hoped, his feedback to each of them was clear—he was thrilled by their performance.

His employee Gordon left Joseph's office. He was the last review for the day. Joseph picked up the phone and called Clarissa, his wife.

"Hey, how's everything going?" she asked.

"Great. I just finished meetings, and it went well."

"No one threw anything at you or argued with you about your criticisms?" she asked, and he could hear the mocking smile through the phone.

"Of course not. I don't know why I was worried about it. It happened once, and I'm always afraid of it happening again. But right now, I've got the best team I could imagine. I have to keep them happy, so they don't disappear."

"They make your job easier, so I'm all for it." There was a brief pause on the line, then Clarissa brought up a new subject. "Hey, I talked to your mom today. They've been looking at where they want to move, and she told me about a place that she liked. I looked into it, and it's a bit on the pricey side."

The couple discussed numbers. He had agreed months ago to help his parents move out of the old home they'd raised him in. His business was going well, and getting them around people their age would be good for their health. And it was the least he could do for all the things they did for him growing up.

By the end of the couple's conversation, Joseph had proved that it was in the budget saying, "I'll tell them to get on the list. They need some community in their life."

"Okay, they'll be thrilled, but your dad will be slow to accept it. "

"Mom can help him with that," Joseph replied.

"Are you headed home soon?"

"Yeah, I'm leaving the office right now."

"Good because Alice is picking out her purpose this afternoon, and she wants you to be there."

"I wouldn't miss it for the world."

***

Alice walked through the door following the shopkeeper with the balloon-shaped nose. She looked at the room full of shelved colorful and shining orbs. There were countless aisles in both directions.

"Help yourself," the shopkeeper said to her as he left her with her parents.

"Alice, one thing," her dad called out.

"What is it, Dad?" She was eager to get started looking at orbs.

He squatted down in front of her, and then picked her up, so she was taller than him or Mom. He let out a long and goofy sigh of exertion.

"Dad, I'm too big for you to pick me up like this," she said behind a smile. She always enjoyed being picked up by him. She saw her mom nod behind him in agreement.

"I just wanted to give you some advice. You don't have to listen to it, but I'd be a bad father if I didn't give you unsolicited advice."

"Yeah, yeah. You're going to tell me what you and mom always tell me. Be generous to others, and try to make them as happy as you." It was a line that she had heard from both her parents multiple times.

"You took the words right out of my mouth. But I want to tell you that for today, and every day from here on, I want you to aim high."

He paused for a moment and looked around. "And look for an orb where you don't have to wear a suit, those are the best ones!"

After that, he hugged her tight and put her back on the ground. With a small piece of paper and a pencil, she darted off, looking at the shelves full of orbs. Each one was a brighter color than the last. There were pinks, purples, blues, greens, and a dozen more.

She picked up an orb with a dark green light that shone through a cloud of smoke. The ball felt cold in her hands as she stared into her first option.

Terrifying Terrain

A scaled reptilian beast crawled over the edge of the mountain and peered down upon the small settlement below. The settlement had landed a week ago, and their goal was to mine and colonize the planet. The Central System's reports didn't list any life on this planet that would hinder those goals. As the monstrosity lumbered through the settlement, crushing the settlement's tents and shuttle, the captain of the mission knew something had been missed on the Central System's reconnaissance.

Shrapnel flew across the town as the power plant the settlers finished building yesterday was kicked by the beast. The captain wondered if the bad intel was intentional sabotage; his political rivals wouldn't like seeing him succeed at starting a colony. The reconnaissance drones sent could potentially have a manufacturing defect, some blind spot to alien life the system was unaware of.

A rogue piece of shrapnel flew across the air toward him. He ran, but as it fell, the shrapnel cut his ankle. Unable to lift himself or take another step, he watched his crewmates scatter in the monster's wake. Each destructive step destroyed something they'd worked to build.

Soon, the settlement was destroyed. What had taken days to build was leveled in an afternoon by this beast. As he watched others bleed out or cry over their lost loved ones, the reptilian beast began making small circles. The pounding of the ground shook underneath the captain as if the tectonic plates of the planet were shifting. After a few minutes, the beast stopped and settled down, curling itself into a ball.

The shape it made was familiar. As he looked at the mountain range on the horizon, he knew humankind would never colonize this planet. If they did, it would have to be void of the mountainous terrain the settlers had hoped to mine.

Descent to the Istalied

T he jets of the boots burned furiously as they lowered Magvon deeper into the cavern. The sporadic light of the jets caught the magnificent crystals embedded into the walls of the cave. His exploration droid floated near him, scanning the intricate system of caverns and creating a map for future records. The map appeared on his heads-up display in bright blue, and he took the paths through the cave that seemed most interesting.

Magvon was one of the many scout researchers sent to survey this exoplanet for valuable discoveries. The exploration of the caverns had eaten away at over half his work cycle, and he needed to head back to the shuttle before it left for the satellite. With each descent further into the cave and the splitting paths he found there, it seemed more and more likely that he would not complete the map during his shift. The droids would have to continue the mapping during his off cycle.

The walls were unlike anything Magvon had seen before. The crystals growing on them dazzled in the light that shone from his helmet and boots. The chemicals the crystals were made of were banal, but the glimmers of them reflected every color of the rainbow. This was likely the first time a light source had graced the cave with its presence, and Magvon was glad he was one of the few people to see its beauty.

Landing on a solid surface that mirrored his helmet's light back into his eyes, he looked up and took in the massive cavern that he'd entered. Every once in a while, the cavern did this. If a colony was set up here, there was no doubt geologists would spend lifetimes studying and theorizing what made these caverns.

As he looked around, he quickly realized this cavern was different. Instead of opening up into a room that could house a shuttle or two, the cavern ended a few meters in front of his face with a dull grey wall. The wall was studded with what appeared to be rivets. The droid flew up and down the wall quickly, surveying the entire cavern as Magvon approached the mysterious wall.

Humans hadn't made it, at least not any humans registered with the Central System. The rivet heads—small palm-sized hemispheres—seemed to float on the surface of the wall. This indicated it was unlikely they were holding something together. It definitely was not human technology. He leaned in close to one as it moved to and fro. As his light searched the wall, the rivets seemed to float away like hair parting from a comb.

A head-splitting scream filled the cavern as he examined the wall, and for a moment, he thought he was the one doing the screaming. He looked around the room for a fellow explorer who might have entered the cave system elsewhere, but he found no one. He looked away from the wall as the earth beneath him began to shake.

Magvon looked for something to cling on to, but everything was shaking around him. This quaking was unsettling, and he wasn't sure what was happening. It was most similar to the botched docking of a shuttle. He wished he could be strapped into a chair, but there was nothing near him. The tumbling of rocks made him cover his head, but it was a pointless action since his arms wouldn't shield him from anything bigger than a pebble.

As suddenly as it started, the quake stopped, and Magvon took in his surroundings. The droid floated through the whole thing and continued to scan the walls. The map showed how the cavern changed by updating to red then fading back to blue. The small hole Magvon had come through turned red. The droid was reporting that boulders now blocked his exit.

Frantically, Magvon scanned the map for alternate entrances to the cavern, hoping that there was some other way out. From the droid's scan, this cavern was a dead end. The density of the rock cut out his suit's communication array hours ago. Since the crew knew communication would be impossible, the droid had enough supplies and thrust to remove him from the cave. The blocked exit was unsettling, but his problem was still solvable.

Using the terminal on his forearm, Magvon began programming the droid to cut through the rock that blocked his path. The machine would make quick work of the obstacle. Soon, he could leave for the shuttle. The crystals in the wall caught the light of the torch as the machine began to execute its new programming.

"Halt!" a voice cried out in a deep rumble that could have caused another quake. Bridges flew from the rivets toward the droid. But the machine dodged out of the way with the help of its AI navigation protocols. The new limbs linked to the rock, further blocking the exit.

"Who's there?" Magvon called out, looking around the small but tall room.

"I am Istalied," the voice replied, "and your presence is disrupting me."

The words Magvon heard weren't coming through the speakers of his headset because they were too loud. The voice seemed to be resonating with his mind. "Where are you? I don't see you?"

There was a long pause until the voice replied, "I am the wall of rivets."

Magvon turned to examine the wall.

"Your presence is disrupting me," the voice repeated. Limbs reached through the rivets and toward Magvon's helmet.

He moved back looking away in horror, but the limbs didn't link to him like they did to the rocks. Looking back hesitantly, he tried to observe the creature without looking directly at it.

He turned to face the creature, and as his light landed on the wall, he watched the rivets begin to grow toward him. "You don't like the light."

"The light disrupts me," the creature said in affirmation.

"What are you?" he asked.

"I am Istalied. I've made this planet my home as I begin my regeneration process."

Magvon began to question the voice further, but before he could, he became a massive organism floating through the cold vacuum of space, absorbing any detritus not held by the gravitational field of a star. He gained nutrients and energy for time unending until he had enough to duplicate himself.

Magvon returned to the dimly lit cavern and reality that he was used to.

"Elder's light," he cursed, "you're in my head... get out!"

He checked his vitals to verify he had not received a head injury during the quake. Calming down as much as he could, he realized the organism was the creature in front of him.

"You're immortal. You've traveled the cosmos since it began."

He waited for a response but didn't receive one. "You can only communicate through my mind," he finally deduced.

"I'll let you enter my mind, but only if you limit your communications to words," he shouted into the dark cavern, making sure to avoid disrupting the monster by looking directly at it.

"You are correct," the Istalied replied.

Magvon began imagining the value this discovery would have. He'd be lauded with praise and accolades for discovering not only a new life form but also a sapient one that had evolved past the point of aging. It would be a groundbreaking discovery, and once the creature was extracted from the planet and studied, humanity would be able to achieve unimaginable feats.

"I will not leave this place until I have regenerated," the voice replied.

Magvon whirled in place, looking directly at the creature, "How'd you know that?"

The limbs pre-emptively bridged from the rivets on the wall as if expecting his turn. They reached out quicker than he could step back, but they did not link to him as they had to the rocks. They stopped centimeters from his light source, mushrooming out and blocking most of the light from passing. They did not block the faceplate of his suit, and with the dim light that reflected off the crystals, he could observe the unsettling beast.

"I said only for communicating with words," Magvon chastised the thing. "Don't take things out of my head." He was unnerved that his mind, the one place that was his own, could be invaded by something so alien.

"It does not work that way. There is only your whole mind. I cannot reach out for only your communication nerves."

"You'll have to leave here eventually for us to study you. You are the first of your kind we've encountered, and it is my job and my duty to report what I've found in these caverns."

"I am the only Istalied in this cosmos; you will not find another one," it explained.

"Then even more reason for us to learn what we can from you. If you're about to go extinct, don't you want to be remembered?"

"Your kind is common," the Istalied replied. "There are more of you surrounding this planet, sending off your incessant electromagnetic and sub-dimensional transmissions, than any of my kind across all the cosmos we inhabit."

Magvon tried to grapple with this fact, but his mind couldn't make sense of it. He felt the creature offer a memory up to help his understanding, but he refused to let it get that far into his mind. He didn't know if it might push him over the edge and into insanity. Assuming he hadn't fallen in already.

Nonetheless, he was in power here since the creature couldn't stand light and he had plenty of that. He could use it to bend the creature to his will. Magvon quickly corralled the thought since the more he focused on it the easier it would be for the Istalied to find it.

"Leave here. I will clear the way for you. Report that there is something dangerous below the surface that makes this a bad place to create a colony," the Istalied explained.

"The droid will cut a way out eventually. And I can use its headlamps to keep you from blocking the way with your limbs again."

"Sapient life in this cosmos is rare," the Istalied stated. "I have no desire to kill you or your kind."

"We don't want to kill you either," Magvon replied, "but we must study you for the good of the Central System and humanity." He wasn't sure how his colleagues would achieve this without light, but that didn't stop him from reprogramming the droid.

The headlights successfully kept the Istalied's limbs from damaging the droid or blocking the rocks. Torches lit to life and made quick work, destroying the rocks that clogged the exit. With all the light being put off, the Istalied's screaming began again.

"Shut up!" Magvon commanded, and the screaming followed a slow decrescendo. He wasn't sure the thing was out of his mind, but the cries of pain had subsided.

The voice then returned, strained by cracks of pain every few words. "Your presence is disturbing me. Your light is disturbing me," it said then repeated the two phrases over and over again.

The statements were unnerving but an improvement over the screaming. And they only completed a few cycles before the blue rocks on his display turned red and disappeared. This left him with a black spot on his map he could escape through.

"Your presence is disturbing me," the voice repeated in his head. And before he could banish the voice all the way out of his mind, he felt it say, "Your light is unnecessary."

Magvon's world disappeared. He couldn't see a thing. Something large fell to the ground and made a *thud*, possibly a dislodged bolder. Feeling the terminal on his hand, he typed in diagnostic commands, but no images appeared on his heads-up display. He must be blind. The thing had entered his mind and made him blind.

"Give me my sight back!" he demanded.

"My electromagnetic pulse cannot damage your nerves," the voice replied coolly. "Life is rare and valuable; I do not wish to kill you."

"I can't see anything," Magvon barked as he flipped emergency switches on the side of his helmet. None of these gave a response. He tried manually lighting the thrusters on his boot heels, but they would not produce a spark of light.

Fumbling around in the dark, he felt the thing that landed in front of him. The texture was smooth and in the shape of the droid's hull. He found each thruster arm and finally the cutting nozzle of the bot. It'd been taken offline as well.

His droid was dead.

His suit was dead.

Echoing through his head were the words, "Your light is unnecessary."

The Ent Colony

2 *6th Serrill 16584 HE*

We land on Yunta tomorrow, and there was a big party on the ship tonight. Mom and Dad gave me this journal and pen as a gift. It's made of paper, and it's like the hand terminal I use for school, but instead of changing files, I flip the pages. They say it's an old thing. They say we'll be using a lot of old things on the colony. But Dad told me many explorers kept journals, so I'll keep one, too.

The party is still happening, I can hear it through the air vents of the ship. Mommy took me to bed, but she let me feel my sister kick in her tummy before I went to sleep. I'm glad she'll be a girl like me; we can go on explorations together when she's older.

Everyone is excited to land tomorrow. I hope that Yunta is more beautiful than the metal walls around me.

***

9th Vilchis 16584 HE

There is so much work to do. Mom can't do much, so I help around the cabin. There is a forest near the village, and every day more logs are hauled into the town. The equipment we brought cuts them into planks or posts. It's loud and dangerous, and Dad says I have to stay away, but in a few years I can use them. Soon, everyone in the colony will have their own house. Dad says we'd never have a house of our own if we stayed in the Central System.

When Mom takes a nap in the afternoon, I sneak away and explore the forest. I imagine I'm a famous explorer like Sacagawea, Armstrong, or Taleeta. So far, I've found twisting rivers and some lizards under rocks. I describe the lizards to Dad, and he says they're common. Biologist found them before we landed.

***

12th Vilchis 16584 HE

We discovered something amazing today. It's all anyone is talking about. I think it discovered us, but the captain is writing to the Central System about it, so I figured I should write about it in my journal. I was about to go exploring when it came lumbering out of the forest. It looked like a tree with bark and leaves growing out of it, but its roots moved slowly across the dirt. The people working on the saws were scared. Some grabbed axes, others ran off for guns. It sat down at the edge of town, its roots digging into the ground. It looked like it'd always been there. It's a little taller than the rest and a little thicker around the trunk. Then it started humming, like the rocket that dropped us off here did when it left. I wanted to be scared, but I'm an explorer, so I approached the saws, getting closer than I was supposed to. Which is why I heard the tree speak.

We all heard its voice in our head like a branch rattling in the wind. It said we were hurting its forest. By then, the captain of the town had come with guns and explained we needed the wood to live. The humming stopped for a while, and my toes felt warm like I was connected to the ground like a tree. The tree hummed again and said it would show us which sick trees and dense areas we could use.

Mom said she didn't hear the voice at the house. She told me to not go into the woods anymore. Dad said the creature was rare. No biologists knew it existed when they first surveyed this planet. I've started thinking of names for it. But maybe I should ask it what its name is. All mine feel silly and made up.

***

15th Vilchis 16584 HE

The wooden giant comes to the village every morning and leads the lumberjacks into the woods. While they cut trees, the captain and doctor ask the giant questions. The captain has had nightly town meetings, reassuring everyone in the town that the giant isn't dangerous. The captain hasn't asked the tree what its name is yet. I keep telling Mom to tell the captain to ask, but she is tired a lot now. She says to Dad that she just wants my sister out.

I still explore the forest a little bit. I hum at the trees and ask if they're awake. None of them have responded yet.

***

26th Vilchis 16584 HE

My sister was born today. Mom and Dad named her Evangeline. It's a long name that's hard to spell, so I call her Eva. Everyone is excited that she's the first Yuntandan. I can hear parties outside, but the doctor said that people should leave our house alone. A lot of people were here to see my mom. She's happy my sister was born, but I can tell she isn't happy with people coming over. She gives them the same look she gives me when I am in the kitchen while she's cooking.

The town meetings are less often, but when we have them, many people complain about not having enough fuel for the winter. We have heat reserves from the ship, but we were mostly counting on the wood to warm us. I remember a story of travelers on the Old World where they had a hard first winter, but the native inhabitants helped them. I hope the wood giant helps us. But the lumberjacks say they're getting less and less wood from the forest every week.

***

3rd Taleeta 16584 HE

Today is our first cold day on Yunta. Boy, is it a chilly one. That's what Dad keeps saying. It was nice yesterday. I was running around barefoot in the grass, but now I'm under the blankets, writing in the living room. Mom has had me watching the fire all day, adding logs when it gets low. The flames are neat to watch, like dancers at Cinderella's ball. My room is too cold so we're all in one room. Eva keeps crying. She's probably keeping the whole village up.

Dad just said it might snow tomorrow. I've never seen snow. Maybe I can play in it or study it. I'll take notes here if it's interesting.

***

4th Taleeta 16584 HE

Snow sucks. Mom says not to use that word, but the lumberjacks use it, and I think it sounds right. Dad found me a warm jacket and boots and pants in the ship's supplies. They're all a bit big, but he says I'll grow into them, and the lumberjacks are complaining all their warm weather gear is too small. But the snow gets everything wet when it touches stuff, and if I press it into a ball like I'm supposed to, it just crushes under my hands. The lumberjacks are having a hard time finding the wood giant. Maybe he hibernates for the winter. So, they started cutting down as many trees as they can, but it's harder than shitting in zero g. That's another thing they say. I don't think I should say it around Mom and Dad though.

***

15th Taleeta 16584 HE

Based on the research survey of this planet, the winter is supposed to stay cold until Mandlestadt. It will probably keep snowing, too. Everyone is always tired and cold, and there are not many parties.

***

20th Taleeta 16584 HE

The wood giant came today and told the lumberjacks that they were taking too much wood from the forest, and they must stop. Dad told me this. I was stuck inside all day, sewing blankets into jackets with Mom so that the lumberjacks will be warmer. I don't like sewing. It's boring, and you miss out on cool stuff like the wood giant showing up.

***

11th Vogelfonte 16584 HE

There is a big blizzard outside. The whole town is in the city hall, and we have a big fire in the fireplace, but I'm still cold. My teeth keep hitting together, and it's annoying. Eva is crying. I want to go home, to the metal ship, and not have to deal with snow or soot or sewing. I want to be able to sleep.

***

Centauri 16584 HE

There were no holiday celebrations even though it's Centauri. Everyone is sleeping in the town hall now. We moved beds in and added another fireplace. Mom, Eva, and I are near the old fireplace, but it's still cold. The lumberjacks can't get more wood. The wood giant is outside our town, and he gives people headaches when they try to sneak into the forest. People talk about killing the wood giant. The captain says we're not allowed to since it's native to the planet.

***

3rd Middleton 16584 HE

I woke up to my mom crying in the middle of night. I'm very sad. I want to go back to the starship. I'd still have a sister if we lived on a starship.

***

7th Middleton 16584 HE

The ground is too cold to bury anyone. The captain is doing something to preserve them. I don't think I want to know what that means because the captain told my dad quietly. Mom is also quiet now.

The lumberjacks talk about sneaking past the wood giant, but they're too slow moving wood back. We've had to start taking down houses and burning them. No one has their own house anyway.

***

4th Mandlestadt 16584 HE

I haven't written in a while because it is sad and boring around the village. There's lots of work to do, and I go to bed tired. I sleep on the same bed as my mom and dad to stay warm. Lots of families do this now. But we won't have to do it much longer. It is warm today, and the snow is melting. I want to go exploring soon. I think I can sneak past the wood giant.

Dad and some other lumberjacks say I might be big enough to work with the saws this year. Mom says I'm still too young, but the lumberjacks need help. And I'm tired of sewing all winter.

***

7th Mandlestadt 16584 HE

The wood giant led us to some trees that didn't wake up from the winter today. I got to go with them; Dad came, too. I tried to help where I could, but everything is too big for me. I stayed out of the way and sat near the wood giant. I asked him lots of questions about the forest and its plants and animals. I also got to ask what his name was. He didn't say anything I understood, but my head filled with the sounds of lizards chirping and water flowing over rocks. I'm glad I know his name, but I don't think anyone will be able to pronounce it. So, I call him Kashoo because it sounds like a lizard chirping and river water.

***

24th Mandlestadt 16584 HE

I talk with Kashoo every day we go into the woods. I don't have much to do. I tie up branches and charge the saw's batteries with solar panels, but it doesn't take me much time. I told Kashoo the story about my mother and Eva. Kashoo wants to be called she and her now because she has a lot in common with my mom's story. I tell Kashoo that if we had more wood then I'd still have a sister. That's what everyone in the town says about the people that are buried in our graveyard. They say colonies shouldn't have graveyards this early and we wouldn't if Kashoo had let us cut down trees. I didn't tell Kashoo all this, just the bit about Eva. Kashoo didn't hum to me the rest of the day. Maybe she's thinking. I hope she's not sad like my mom now.

***

27th Mandlestadt 16584 HE

Kashoo talked to me again today. She said I was the only person who loved the forest like her. I said I didn't think that was true, but she says the lumberjacks just treat the forest like it's a commodity, but I am curious and ask questions about how it works. She asks me if I can do something to stop them. I told her I'm not important enough to do that.

I talked to Dad about it. I feel like a famous explorer who discovered something important, but he told me not to talk to Kashoo anymore. Only the captain is allowed to.

***

Elder's Day 16584 HE

The captain and Kashoo fight a lot now. I hear about it in the town hall where we still sleep. We haven't gotten enough wood to rebuild our houses, and we're working to store up fuel. People are talking about getting rid of Kashoo, like she's just another tree in the forest. I asked Mom if they're going to do this. I was crying, and she patted my back. Eventually, Dad explained that it's not allowed because the Central System exists to protect sapient life. If the lumberjacks hurt Kashoo, they'd be in a lot of trouble. Some say that they'll be in trouble next winter if they don't do it. The captain has requested researchers and extra funding that he can spend on fuel and equipment. I hope the researchers can figure out how to balance Kashoo's needs and the needs of the village.

***

13th Stein 16584 HE

I think we should leave. I snuck off and spoke to Kashoo this afternoon and told her about the researchers. That made her scared, and

I'm sorry I told her, but I just wanted to help. I didn't tell her about what the lumberjacks wanted to do. But they don't hide their feelings. I think she can tell what they want while they work.

I asked Dad why we couldn't just leave, and he said there weren't many planets that humans could live on. Yunta is special like that, and if the human race is going to survive, we need planets like this. I asked if Kashoo would be able to survive here, too. He said the researchers would figure something out.

***

15th Stein 16584 HE

The captain announced that the researchers would be here in two weeks. We just got our first message from them, and the captain is sending them his notes. I asked Dad if I should send them mine, and he thought the captain would be able to do it without my help. I've started typing things up on my old terminal anyway.

***

4th Acrecia 16584 HE

I snuck off and told Kashoo that the researchers were coming tomorrow. She was soaking her roots in a river while lizards crawled between them. She told me that I should do what I can to protect the forest. I said I wasn't that important. I wasn't a big tree like her. But she told me that there were little bugs and fungus that broke down dead trees into dirt and that's an important part of taking care of the forest.

I got back later than usual. There was a big fight between the captain and the lumberjacks outside the town hall. Mom was glad I was home, and she made me eat dinner and go to sleep early "before anything crazy happened." Those were the words she used. But crazy things always happen around here.

***

5th Acrecia 16584 HE

The researchers got here today. I couldn't talk to them because they were busy with the captain. I sent them my write up on Kashoo. Mom helped me with some of the spelling, and it may not be perfect, but it should show them I know a lot about her.

***

7th Acrecia 16584 HE

The researchers can't find Kashoo. She hasn't been to the village since I last saw her. The lumberjacks are cutting as many trees down as they can. If Kashoo comes back, she will be very angry. But I don't think she'll be back. I hope she found a faraway forest. Maybe one we can't find, hidden away like Neverland.

Swinging Sticks

The house they put me in was just this side of falling apart. I'd had nicer apartments and worse ones. It was still serviceable, but if I didn't get done what I'd come here to do, I would wind up becoming a repairman, not something I was well suited for.

The house sat in a place outside of time and space. It had taken me nearly a decade to save up enough money to get here, and I had one purpose: write and finish at least one great novel. Which I would soon find was not as simple as I'd originally expected.

The first floor had a sitting room, void of a television and radio, but plenty of paintings on the walls. Although they were too realistic for my liking. The pantry was stocked with countless canned foods and staples that were bound to last a lifetime. The refrigerator had no shortage of fresh options available to me there.

When I walked up the stairs, the second step from the top creaked every time I stepped on it, and the sound echoed through the vacuous house. There were two bedrooms on the second floor, neither of which were large. One held a single bed, a dresser with black and gray shirts, and a nightstand with a small stained glass lamp on it.

The room across the hall held a heavy wooden desk with ornate carvings from the clawed feet to the vines that seemed to grow around the edges. The polished wood top was vacant with the exception of an old-fashioned typewriter. No embedded terminal, no microphone for voice transcribing; they didn't even go as low tech as an ancient desktop computer tower. The typewriter didn't plug into the wall and couldn't connect to a network, even if there was one in this pocket dimension. The drawers held a number of pens, pencils, quills, and paintbrushes. A few reams of paper sat in the bottom desk drawer, the sturdy wood unwilling to buckle under the weight of the paper.

A bookshelf loomed behind the desk, carved just as intricately. The books, most of which I'd requested to be there for reference or inspiration, had genuine paper pages with stiff covers. A shelf alone would have covered the cost of my entrance into this place. And I let the thin pages flutter across my thumb as I looked them over.

Vogelfonte Inc. specializes in the creation, maintenance, and transportation to sub-dimensional pockets of existence. It was proprietary technology that Augustus Vogelfonte discovered, and its usage varies from military training to creative retreats and is marketed to multiple sectors and conglomerates that are interested in advancement and improvement. No one outside the company knows how it works, least of all me, a writer of, at best, space station dramas.

Until recently, I worked as a logistical engineer for the Acrecia conglomerate, which handled the food distribution to most major systems. It was about as creative a pursuit as buff-cow herding, and even then, I may not be giving the ranchers enough credit. It paid me just a little more than my expenses, but I worked to stash away enough to take out a loan on a Vogelfonte sub-dimensional creative retreat. I got a discount by sharing the sub-dimension with another person, a decision I would soon come to regret. But I was outside of time, and the loan would not accrue interest until I finished the book, which if it was good enough, would cover the loan's amount, and I'd be out of debt and able to make a living as a writer.

And if it wasn't good enough, I would simply stay here until I made it good enough. I was in a place where time moved infinitesimally slower than time in the real world. Life extension drugs—included in my purchase—could reset me to my current age if I felt the need to spend lifetimes here. This house was, or at least should have been, a paradise.

Which was why it was confusing to me when I stepped outside and all that I could see was sand. The exception being the nearly identical house that sat a half dozen meters away. The images on Vogelfonte's marketing material always showed island paradises, or forested retreats, with famous writers relaxing with a pen and paper in their hands. I opted for the same, or at least similar, reality as the one Alexandra Hardy used to write her breakout masterpiece *The Moons of Her Eyes*. How she got something done in such a wasteland was a mystery to me, which I guess explained the lower package price despite the success associated with the location.

A weathered rocking chair sat on the porch and stared at the sandy horizon. It was unclear which was more uncomfortable, the hard wooden chair or the empty expanse of the horizon. Both were un-settling, so I decided that a hot and fresh meal would spark some inspiration. Preparing my own meal wouldn't be too hard. Humans have been doing it for generations, and it may be a good exercise in creativity.

I found some chicken thighs sealed tight in a bag in the refrigerator. Zucchini and broccoli were sitting in a drawer. I cut them into a variety of sizes, then gathered the most interesting sounding spices from the pantry. I planned to put together a stir fry. It seemed easy enough. After all, the instructions were in the name. It was my favorite meal, so

I had plenty of experience eating it. Cooking has never been my strong suit, never needed to be since there were plenty of units to prepare meals for me in all my apartments.

Quickly, I realized that this was not as simple as the automation robots made it seem. To make matters worse, the pan was flimsy, the spatula was bent, and the burner was just an electric coil. I'm not one who could appreciate high quality tools, but these surely weren't doing me any favors. Nonetheless, the food wound up on the plate, and the charred bits of meat made me confident it was done.

There was another serving still in the pan after filling a bowl to the brim, so I made a second bowl to take to the neighbor. Sticking a fork, chopsticks, and spoon into the rice, unsure of how they might like to eat it, I made my way across the few meters of sand with the piping hot bowls in my hands.

I heard someone shout "one minute," after hitting the doorbell with my elbow. Peeking through the windows, I noticed the layout was a mirror image of mine.

The door opened, and a man in a loosely tied bathrobe greeted me with hair so chaotic that I thought it'd jump off his scalp to attack me. "I'm your new neighbor," I said, introducing myself and offering him my lunch, likely his breakfast.

"Doug Smith," he replied, taking the stir fry out of my hand and gesturing me inside.

We sat at the small table, which was identical to the one in my house, and I took a bite of my meal. After removing the spare utensils out of his, Doug took a bite and immediately said, "This is utterly disgusting!"

I couldn't disagree with him. The flavor was nothing like the N-Ector versions of the meal, and despite burning the outside to a crisp, there were still pieces of meat that were raw on the inside. Nonetheless,

I didn't appreciate his candor and continued to eat my portion out of spite. He cracked open a can of beans and warmed them on the stove as I started a conversation. "So what are you working on here?"

"I'm a musician," he said while stirring the beans in the bowl.

"What do you play?"

"Drums." He punctuated the statement by twirling his spoon between his fingers. It immediately clattered to the ground. Picking it up, he wiped the round end with his robe, placing a bean stain next to a dozen similar ones.

"That's exciting." And not knowing much about drums, or musicians in general, I said, "I'm a writer. I'm working on a novel."

He tasted the beans out of the bowl and decided they were warm enough and rejoined me at the table. "Don't you think there's enough of those already?"

"Which? Writers or novels?"

"Either," he said with a shrug. "Hasn't every story already been written? When I watched the net back home there were a dozen different space station noir shows. You can't tell me every one of those episodes is significantly different from the rest."

I didn't know how to respond at first. Formulaic dramas were nothing like the novel I planned to create. "Sure, there are similar themes and structures between stories, but our lives in the stars are far different from the mono-planet writers we inherited them from. And besides, haven't all the drums been beaten?"

"That's completely different," he said as he chewed a mouthful of beans. "Drums were made to be changed into different patterns, and there's value in me practicing existing music so that I can replicate it live. Not to mention drums are cool. Novels... that's just crap they make you read in school."

Fuming at the comparison, I could tell that his passion for the point would overcome any logic I tried to apply. I steered the conversation to his life before entering this sub-dimension. He was happy to share this information with me between bites of beans and eventually a mouth full of peaches plucked straight from their can.

As I scraped out the last bit of stir fry from the dish, a limp piece of zucchini, Doug said, "You know you don't have to mess with cooking that stuff." It was followed by an insufferable slurping sound as he drank the juice from the peach can. "Just eat the canned stuff; you only need to eat to keep your energy up."

"I mostly did it to give cooking a try."

"Well, I hope you're a better writer than a chef, otherwise you'll be here until the place folds in on itself."

"That's a thing that can happen?" I asked, concerned and trying to figure out if it was mentioned on one of the forms I signed after a quick skim.

He gave a hearty chuckle and said, "No, it's a turn of phrase. My turn of phrase. But if you want to use it you can."

I politely kept to myself the opinion that his phrase wasn't suited for any work of fiction or non-fiction I'd ever write. I soon worked my way out of the conversation by saying that I needed to get to writing before the day was over, and I wished him luck with his drum practice.

***

Sitting at the desk, I followed some printed instructions and eventually got the hang of using the typewriter. It was nearly as finicky as a word processor. I would align the paper exactly where I wanted the strikers to land, begin to type out the title of the novel, and it would somehow not be centered. After going through a dozen pieces of paper, I finally had the title "Giants Among Us" centered perfectly with my name underneath it. Rolling in a new blank piece of paper, everything was ready to begin my manuscript.

Doug had been so wildly lost on the subject of how creative writing could be. I had dozens of more options than he had drums, and I could combine each one to make countless words, then those made countless sentences, and then countless stories. Sure, stories shared some patterns and themes across the ages, and yes, space station noirs on the net could be repetitive. But this novel I had planned—a beautiful story about a fortune teller knowing her future husband was going to die of a brain disease then falling in love with him anyway—was like nothing else I'd ever read.

I looked over the keys, unsure of which letter to use first. The opening line had to be perfect, jaw-dropping, and gripping. I knew it had to give the reader enough to get into the story without disclosing everything. I wondered if I should start with the character's name, and I tried to find one that would suit her. Then I decided to write it in first person which settled that... for now. Since she was a fortune teller, I considered starting with a vision of the future, or maybe a flashback. As I worked to make the timeline come together in my head, something grabbed my stomach.

There should be medicine in the house to reduce my anxiety. My stomach began turning inside out, and I rushed to the bathroom, realizing that this wasn't the result of my anxiety.

Clutching the edges of the toilet, I ejected my lunch into the bowl. Saying that something in it didn't agree with me was an understatement. I kept retching even after I felt like I didn't have anything left inside me. Finally, I laid on the bathroom floor, defeated. I felt awful, and as soon as I could make it to bed, I vowed I'd lay there until my strength returned. No more writing would get done today.

I crawled into bed. The springs and metal posts creaked against each other. The mattress was unremarkable. Good enough to get a night's sleep but no zero-g sleep system. I groaned and wrestled with my stomach, which was now unhappy about something new despite being emptied. I didn't think I would ever fall asleep, but I must have because Doug's drum practice startled me awake.

I squinted at the clock. Its confusing arms gestured at two and twelve. I rolled over and found a pillow to cover my ears, hoping that Doug would only practice for a few minutes before going to bed. The pillow did little to help, and the drums continued for what felt like hours. By the time he finished, the morning light was creeping in through the window curtains.

I cannot sleep with a single ray of light in my room. I've always had artificial windows in my space station apartments, ones I could turn on and off at my whim. And the blinds of this house were doing little more than keeping prying eyes out. The light would only worsen as the morning dragged on, so I gave up and stumbled downstairs.

I milled around the house for the rest of the morning, trying baked beans I had to bake again, and refried beans which didn't benefit from a second frying. The canned fruits lacked the crispness of ones grown in the hydroponic farms. That, combined with my experience last night, made me hate just about everything I tasted.

Exhausted, I tried reading some of the books that were on the shelf. Unfortunately, the ones I'd read before didn't excite me, and the ones that were new to me didn't pull me in quick enough. Tired of trying to distract myself and hopeless that I'd get back to sleep, I sat down at the typewriter.

I typed the letter "I" on the first page, hoping it would inspire me. After all, I'd unintentionally read a dozen opening lines in an attempt to find something interesting to read. The rest of the words for the hook came to me, and I began to type the sentence out.

Every third letter typed, the machine replied with an unsettling scraping sound. I slowly typed the line's subsequent letters, watching the strikers swing up from where they rested, trying to find where the sound came from. It was unbearable to listen to, and if I were to write tens of thousands of words on this thing, it would be torture. I stopped mid-sentence and rummaged through the desk drawers to find something that might keep the thing from scraping. The drawers were void of any oil or tools, and I began pushing pens into the machine to see if I could realign its parts. A few characters later, I'd forgotten how I'd worded the rest of the sentence in my head. I let out a frustrated cry and went downstairs to keep myself from throwing the cursed thing out the window.

Pacing back and forth between the living room and dining room, I noticed a new sound that also seemed incessant. It was coming from the kitchen, and I moved around like a cat to see if I could hunt down the source of the noise. The culprit was soon apparent. The refrigerator made a constant whirring sound I hadn't noticed yesterday. Living on space stations, I'd grown accustomed to background hums and mechanical vibration. But I'd paid a good sum of money to live in this house in peace and quiet. And this refrigerator was making a sound I couldn't ignore.

Searching the house, I found a small bag of tools. I am no mechanic. I barely know where the ship dock is in any given station I've lived on. I pass through it when traveling and then forget its location until I need to leave. Any issue I've ever found in my living quarters required me to contact a licensed professional. Otherwise, I was likely to put a hole in something I wasn't supposed to and space myself and potentially everyone else on the station. Here, I didn't have that restraint. So, I began disassembling the refrigerator to stop the sound.

I twisted what I could, having a hard time finding the right tool, assuming it existed, and it was in the small tool bag. I fiddled with this project for a while, much longer than I tried my hand at cooking. Nonetheless, I enjoyed working on something and understood how some people could find a job like this rewarding. I began imagining the various mechanic characters I might work into my novel, trying to diverge from determined not to use the awful cliches. Finally, I wiggled a bit of the fridge's wiring that must have been out of place, and it silenced the machine.

My casual button-up shirt was covered in sweat. Walking around the house, I searched for a cool spot. I found a vent that was supposed to be sending fresh air into the house. However, it wasn't doing a great job. The afternoon sun had beaten its way into this place, and my air conditioning was unable to defend against it. I made a mental note to myself to use my newfound mechanic skills to work on that next.

I sat on the couch, exhausted, but the cloth seemed to absorb my sweat, keeping me from cooling down, so I migrated to a stiff kitchen chair. Unfortunately, it was near the sunniest window in the house. I finally lay down on the rough hardwood floor, and the cool air that sat on the floor helped me regulate my body temperature.

The refrigerator no longer hummed, and when my strength returned, I pushed it into place, removing a crispy green apple from the contraption. Exhausted from the lack of sleep and the amount of work I'd put into today, I sat on the porch now that the sun was making its way behind the horizon.

Rocking back and forth in the primitive wooden chair, I looked over to Doug's house and saw he was doing something similar. He had a beer in one hand and was playing some music through an old-style speaker system. I was glad the music didn't reach much past his porch since it was the raucous and chaotic rock 'n roll that every station's dive felt the need to play. I considered visiting him on his porch, but the conversation we'd shared last time was memorable in all the wrong ways. The day had been quiet, and I wondered if he'd been as uninspired as me today. Surely the middle of the night practice sessions weren't regular occurrences.

***

Doug might as well be using my head for a drum. His music crashed through my ears all morning. Pillows and covers did little to drown out the noise. It'd been a week of incessant 2:00 AM drum practice leaving me hopelessly exhausted. I'd done little to no writing since arriving at this house. As consolation for putting up with his racket, I climbed out of bed for some ice cream.

For the past few days, the kitchen had a distinct odor. I always knew my cleaning wasn't up to par with the housekeeper bots installed in modern apartments, but the room was practically spotless. I opened the fridge, and a pungent smell slapped me in the face.

I quickly closed the door, but it was too late. For the past week, I begrudgingly followed Doug's advice and focused on eating canned food, as awful as it was. And since the refrigerator wasn't making a racket, I'd ignored it. Holding my nose and inspecting it further, I realized the box wasn't cold like it should've been. All the food was rancid, and the contents would only be valuable to biologists interested in studying the new species of mold inhabiting it.

Suited up in thick rubber gloves and a kitchen apron, I carried as much as I could to the house's recycler to be transported to some other sub-dimension or out of existence altogether. I didn't care as long as the smell wasn't abusing my nose.

I wrote a letter on Voglefonte-branded stationery, requesting more refrigerated food, and dropped it in the old-fashioned mailbox. The folks in charge of my experience would soon generate more food into my fridge. Before that happened, I needed to repair the thing. I undid my wiring repair until the thing began to make a racket again. I finished around the time Doug wrapped up his practicing. The silence I desired seemed to always evade me.

Sitting on the couch in an oversized shirt and loose shorts, I listened to the constant humming of the fridge. It was less erratic than Doug's performance but no more enjoyable. I wondered what the neighbor was doing, and I'm ashamed to admit that I went upstairs to peek out my window to see if I could see any movement in his house.

The curtains of his window were wide open. Doug lay passed out on his bed in nothing more than his underwear, unafflicted with the light sensitivity problem I was cursed with. Embarrassed to have viewed such a private moment, I closed my window curtain and went to the office to write.

The words came to me slowly, if at all, just like every other morning Doug's drumming woke me up. Staring at the typewriter, I thought of how I could bring up rescheduling his practice time, instead of what my characters might be doing. The most confrontational thing I'd done was write a politely worded message to a coworker, and I did not think that approach would go far with Doug.

I am not one to knock on my neighbor's door while they're sleeping, studying, or practicing. Nor would I bother them at night. Doug's schedule meant that I'd have to violate at least one of those things, which I would never appreciate someone doing to me. And so, I kept to my own house, hoping that Doug would soon master the drums so that I could begin writing my novel.

That delusion worked for a while, until I had to go over to Doug's house for his own safety.

***

I woke up naturally at about a quarter to two, and I rolled over to go back to sleep. Knowing that drum practice was imminent kept me up. When silence still lingered in the house at a quarter to three, I knew something was wrong with Doug.

We are not simulated in these sub-dimensions. It's not some clunky virtual reality where your body is still in another world and your perception is the only thing that's moved. The Vogelfonte conglomerate moves our body here, and if we die here, we die in real life. I was confident in this fact above all other facts because I'd signed copious documents acknowledging that I was aware of it.

Meaning if Doug was in trouble, it was my responsibility as his neighbor to make sure that he was removed from this world before anything fatal happened. I would expect Doug, and everyone I'd ever shared a space station with, to do the same for me. Because despite all the life-extending drugs humanity has, we've yet to recombine bodies with their consciousness.

I lurked into his house. The front door was open. After all, I was the only person who could rob his stockpile of beans, and his supply matched mine.

There was no one on the first floor, so I proceeded to the second floor. His stairs creaked as much as mine did. Calling out for Doug didn't return any acknowledgment, and so I continued into the bedroom. The bed was a mess, and clothes were piled high on the floor. The dresser, bedside table, and even the bed's headboard had kitchen pots and empty cans littered across them. A beat cop from a space station noir might classify this as a sign of a struggle, but I suspected it was Doug's way of life.

Crossing the hall to his study, I cracked the door open, unsure of what I would find, and I hoped Doug was conscious or at least his organs were still working. I peeked through the slit of the door. At first, the sight in front of me confused me, but once I gathered what was going on, I stumbled away in desperation.

Doug sat on a round stool surrounded by drums and cymbals of various sizes. Each drum had a hole or split in the taught plastic cover. None of them made a sound as he whacked his stick against it. Despite the damaged equipment, he still swung his sticks wildly through the air, hitting the drums despite their mute response. The cymbals lay on the ground, their broken stands leaning against the wall. Despite this, he still beat his sticks onto the site where the cymbals would have perched. Doug, not exactly humanity's finest specimen, was completely mad. And I made the mistake of intruding into his den.

As I backed away, I tripped on a loose pan. I fell to the ground with a loud clatter. Doug swiveled around in his stool and saw me laying on the ground.

"I was trying really hard to ignore you," he groaned, "but you don't make it easy. Did you come to see why there was no ballad tonight?" His mouth was crooked with a smile that sent a chill down my spine.

"I... I just... I just wanted to make sure you were okay."

Doug cackled. "Right as rain."

"Your drums don't work," I pointed out. Mostly to make sure I was still the sane one in this interaction.

He shrugged and twirled a drumstick between his fingers with more success than he'd had with the spoon. "They work as well as they ever have," he assured me.

Glad that he'd confirmed my sanity, I said,. "They're all busted and not making noise."

"Oh," he said as if I'd just explained the answer to a riddle. "The sticks still work. And I've got a dozen more of these."

"But you're not making a sound," I protested, despite being glad for the silence.

"I'm not here to make sound," he said in a tone I hadn't heard since graduating school. "I'm here to swing sticks." He presented the sticks to me, found a crack in one, and snapped it in half, tossing it onto a pile of similar sticks. "Now, if you don't mind, I am going to get back to work. After all, I don't interrupt you while you're writing."

I began to protest, but he swept his fingers at me in a gesture to get going. I backed out politely, closing the door behind me. As I walked down the stairs, I heard him call out, "Don't worry, I'll order new drumheads in the morning, so the performances will return tomorrow."

I don't know if my groan reached back up the stairs, and I don't think Doug would have cared if it had.

Frustrated by the absurdity of the night, I lay in bed, hoping the silence would help me to sleep. But no, I was like an acclimated third shift worker unable to stay awake during the day cycle. I gave up sooner than expected and dragged myself across the hall into my office.

Sitting in front of the typewriter, I began to swing my sticks. My fingers picked keys at random, adding ink to the page. Soon, I reached the end of the page, so I rolled it back to the first line and typed over the previous characters.

I kept punching keys, looking forward to the scraping that happened to every third key—resetting the page to the header before it fell out the back. I used up all the ribbon's ink and watched the strikers stamp the black page with faint imprints of the letters. Doug's ridiculous practice had cursed me with wakefulness. I might as well play along with the same absurd disinterest he had of the outcome.

The sun eventually rose and beat through the window curtains. Daylight delivered some practicality, or as much as there was to be had here. I took the marred and stained paper out of the typewriter and pinned it on the wall.

I replaced the ribbon and rolled a fresh piece of paper into the machine. I knew how to swing my sticks without losing focus, so I began writing a story. Not one where the plot was undiscovered and characters had yet to receive names. I typed out a story I knew by heart because I'd just lived it. And it began with a house just this side of falling apart.

The story I wrote that day was garbage, and it's been garbage the past three times I've written it. One day, it might be decent enough to let someone read, but for now, I merely type the story out, stack the page, and load in the next blank one. After a few more sentences, I'll sit on the porch and look out to the sandy horizon of this wasteland. I'll go about my day, breaking or fixing things as needed, and then get to bed early so I can be well-rested.

Tomorrow will begin as it always does, with a racket early in the morning, reminding me to swing my sticks.

* * *

Looking for More to Read?

I have one more story that I couldn't fit into this anthology. "Boulders in the Stream" is about a rogue human colony discovered by the Central System and the clash of different societies.

You can download it for free here: https://stepintotheroad.com/free-short-story/

***

Reviews are very important for independent authors like me. If you enjoyed The Path of the Bearer and Other Stories, please consider leaving a review. Even simple, one-line reviews are very helpful to indie authors. Thank you for your support!

Also By Nicholas Licalsi

An Echo Through Time

T odd can travel through time and the multiverse. With a single focused breath, he can be any place and any time.

Instead, he relives the same day of high school over and over, knowing his sweetheart will die by lunch.

And there's nothing he can do to save her.

Equipped with time travel Todd rarely feels powerless, but his sweetheart's deaths make him question his place in the multiverse.

If you enjoy thrilling time travel stories An Echo Through Time will have you on the edge of your seat!

https://books2read.com/EchoThroughTime

Bleeding Rock

Mauve, a talented mechanic, always dreamed of leaving her satellite home. So she didn't think twice before signing up for a routine planetary survey.

Mauve awakes from the landing hanging upside down. Clearly something went wrong. She will need all her mechanical knowledge to get the mission back on track.

But the crash landing is only the start of her troubles.

With her AI assistant Mauve must use everything she discovers on this alien world to escape it.

If you enjoy science fiction exploration stories with elements of horror then you'll love Bleeding Rock!

https://books2read.com/BleedingRock

A Trial of Rock and Rope

Upon his death, Ferrun Monteiro wakes up in the afterlife. Instead of building paradise the gods have designed a challenge.

To escape the afterlife Ferrun must reach the top of a mountain with a boulder tied to his ankle.

Yet not a single soul has completed this seemingly simple trial.

Unperturbed, Ferrun faces the god's challenge head on. Follow him on his odyssey through the afterlife.

If you enjoy dreaming about the afterlife, you'll enjoy A Trial of Rock and Rope.

https://books2read.com/ATrialOfRockAndRope

About the Author

Nicholas Licalsi was born and raised outside of Fort Worth, in the beautiful but backwards state of Texas. Growing up, he was fascinated with science fiction and fantasy. This interest led to pursuing a degree in engineering and participating in multiple robotics competitions. After a successful enough career in software development Nicholas spends his time trying to trick his overactive imagination into paying the bills while he satiates his dog's need to be pet.

You can connect with me at: https://stepintotheroad.com

Get updates about my upcoming books at: https://stepintoth eroad.com/signup